CHILDREN OF THE DEAD

HANNAH SARAH ABRAHAM

Made with ♥ on the Notion Press Platform
www.notionpress.com

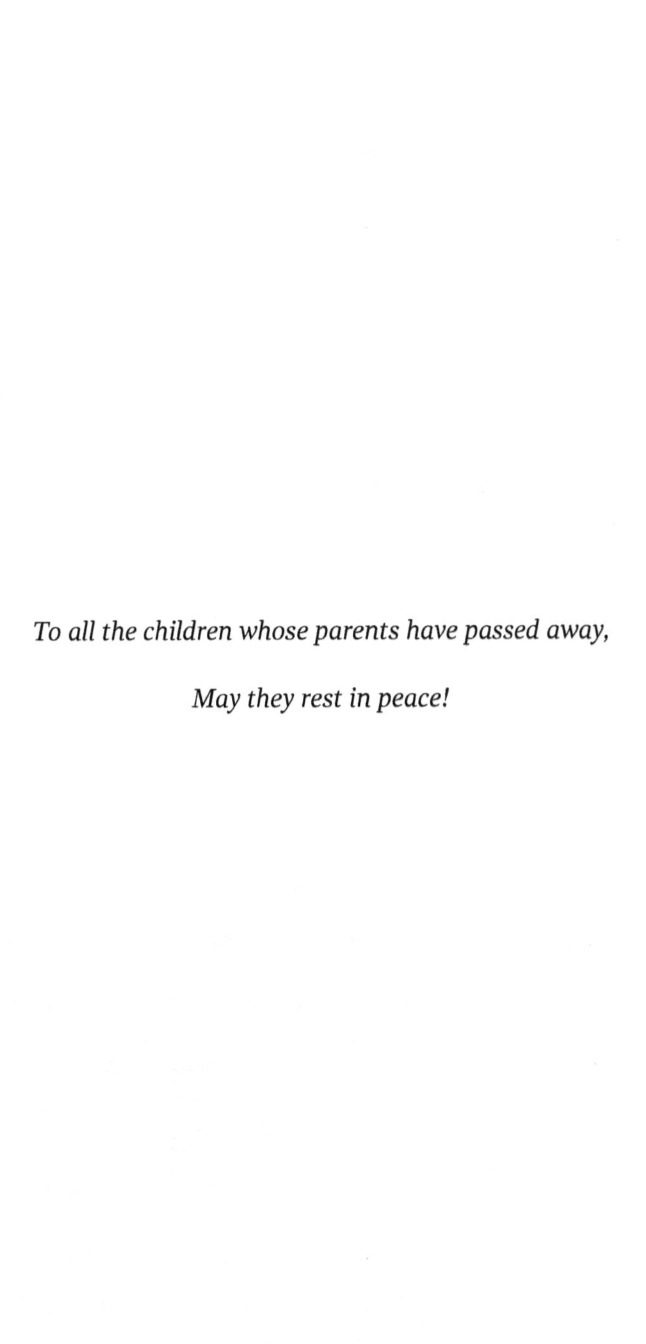

To all the children whose parents have passed away,

May they rest in peace!

Contents

Contents

Preface

Dear Readers,

To be completely candid, I often get my inspiration to write novels when I listen to songs. I am certain readers who enjoy reading thriller/mystery/crime novels will devour this book. I can assure you, you won't have dry eyes after you are done reading this story. I'll admit, I felt a bit blue after writing this book. This novel tugged at my heartstrings and my chest felt heavy after reading the last line. I wish it will have the same effect on you as it did on me. A lot of tears and sleepless nights went into crafting this novel. Hope you will enjoy the fruits of my hard labour.

Happy reading!

With love,

Hannah

Acknowledgements

Alan Walker's song *Faded* is the primary source of inspiration for my novel *Children of The Dead.*

A special thanks to my Dad who constantly encouraged me to pursue writing and never give up.

Thanks to my furry friends, Chloé and Cassie, for giving me the emotional support I needed to write this novel.

Lastly, thanks Mom, for supporting me and believing in me when no one else did.

Disclaimer

This is a work of fiction. Unless otherwise indicated, all the names, characters, businesses, places, events, and incidents in this book are either the product of the author's imagination or used in a fictitious manner. Any resemblance to actual persons, living or dead, or actual events is purely coincidental.

Trigger Warning

This novel contains graphic depictions of violence, bloodshed, gore, physical and emotional abuse, self-harm, nudity, depictions of sexual intimacy, sexual assault and murder.

It's only meant to be read by those 18 years and older.

A Lament By Giulia

The Living Dead
"Most of us are definite of the fine lines between the
living and the lifeless.
A dual of life and death blossom'd in me a bitter-sweet
nothingness.
I'm nothing but a frail form clothed in covers of
oblivion,
Carrying countless emotions;
Those of which are sound in my still heart
That hold hues of black and white, part and part
Unable to paint my very presence in monochrome
Not an inkling of how people perceive my duplexity
This burning desperation in my core to make my
hopeless existence an actuality.
Am I a pale impersonation of the living; an inexact
depiction of the dead
Or a living embodiment of the dead?
It all seems rather riveting than rational in the end."
By Giulia Moretti

Prologue

Luca went to his study, and I went to his bedroom. Luca didn't find suspicious anything in his study. I found a bible and a rosary on his bedside table. But when I flipped through the pages of the Bible, a letter fell out of one of the pages of the Bible. I picked it up and gasped loudly.

"Luca, look what I found in his bedroom," I said, waving the letter in his face.

Luca rushed to the study, panting.

"What is it?" Luca asked, breathless.

My hands were trembling as I read the letter aloud.

"Dear Giulia,

I miss you, dear. Your piercing blue eyes, your lovely smile, your beautiful golden hair, your plump lips, your smooth skin, and your pure white frock. I miss all of you."

I'm praying to God for your safe return. Daddy is waiting for his little girl to come back home.

Love,

Rev. James"

Part One (Laura Moretti)

CHAPTER ONE

THE STRANGE DISAPPEARANCE OF GIULIA

"For all have sinned, and fall short of the glory of God." *(Romans 3:23)*

It has been more than six months since I last saw my twin sister. Her name is Giulia. She is so much prettier than me. I've always envied how beautiful she looks in her pure white frock.

All the girls in the children's home are required to wear starched white frocks because our matron, Miss Maria, says that it symbolizes our chastity. I didn't even know what that word meant. I once asked the matron what the word 'chastity' meant. She told me it means 'sexual purity.' She said sexual purity involves no kissing, no touching, and no sex with someone of the opposite gender. When I asked her what sex meant, the matron got furious and asked me to recite *Hail Mary* and *The Lord's Prayer* fifty times. She also told me that I was not to eat dinner that night. I was starving myself to death in my room when Luca, one of the boys in the children's home, snuck into my room and offered me some meatloaf and a peach cobbler. I gobbled them down in one bite. I still remember the smile on his face when he watched me wolf down the food.

I was never fond of wearing the white frock that our matron forces us to wear. I like wearing colourful frocks. I once got in deep trouble when I wore a beautiful blue and white polka-dotted frock. The matron told me I had sinned against the Lord and that I was tempting the boys to stray away from the Lord. I still don't understand what was so "tempting" about my blue and white polka-dotted frock. I was always getting on the bad side of the matron, unlike my sister who was always on her good side. I hated her for that!

But now I don't hate her, I'm worried about her. I really miss her and I would do anything to see her again. At this point, I'm not even sure if she is alive. The matron says that my sister eloped with the gardener working on our estate. It's not like her to run away with someone on a whim. Besides, the gardener is not even that good-looking. He looks like a total creep! Rumour has it that the gardener was paid a huge sum by the matron to stay away from the children's home for as long as possible. Everyone at St. Agnes children's home gossips about my sister and it breaks my heart. They all hate her, except Luca. He is the only one who believes that my sister is innocent and that she didn't run away with the gardener.

One day, the matron told me that she caught Giulia having sex with the gardener behind the children's home about eight months ago. I told her I still didn't know what "sex" meant. The matron told me it was when a man does "something bad" to a woman's body. Could she get any vaguer than that? She said it was to rob a girl or woman of her innocence and sexual purity. "It's an act of vicious theft," she said. I've been scared of sex ever since. That day, I vowed to never have sex ever in my life.

When the matron told me about sex, I was both frightened and fascinated by it. If the matron was not going to tell me what exactly it was, then I was going to find the meaning elsewhere.

After I left the matron's room, I called Luca to my room and asked him what sex meant. Luca stared at me for a while and then blushed. He seemed to know a thing or two about sex.

"Are you sure you want to know what sex means?" Luca asked, his face turning redder and redder.

"Yes," I said, curtly.

"It is the act of a penis penetrating a vagina," Luca said, inserting a finger between his index finger and thumb.

"What's a penis and a vagina?" I asked with a blank look on my face.

"You have a vagina and I have a penis," Luca said, pointing at my nether region.

"What is the point of sex?" I asked, frowning.

"When a penis penetrates a vagina, a baby is made," Luca said, cradling an imaginary baby in his arms.

"What, really?" I asked with a surprised look on my face.

"Yeah...."

"I wonder what's it like to have sex," I said, stroking my chin.

"I have a picture of two people having sex. Do you wanna see it?" Luca murmured.

"Yes," I said, nodding my head.

Luca pulled out an old picture from a storybook. The man was sitting on top of the woman. They were completely naked like Adam and Eve. It looked like the man was hurting the woman with his penis. I couldn't stop staring at it. It was the moment I lost my innocence forever.

"Does the matron know about the picture?" I muttered under my breath.

"No way! She would kill me if she saw this," Luca said, shuddering.

"Who gave this picture to you?" I asked with a curious countenance.

"Reverend James."

"The pastor in our parish?" I asked, raising my eyebrows.

"Yup."

"Why would he give you this?" I asked, scratching my head.

"He told me that there are certain things a man will come across in his life and that it's best if I knew about them from him."

"You think the pastor has sex?" I asked, lost in thought.

"As a Catholic, the pastor is forbidden to have sex. His body is the temple of God, the instrument of Christ, and the vessel of the Holy Spirit."

"You think the pastor wants to have sex?" I asked, my heart hammering in my chest.

"Maybe. Why else would he give me this picture?" Luca said, shrugging.

"Should we tell the matron about him?" I asked, shifting my weight from one foot to the other.

"No. He'll get in trouble," Luca said with pleading eyes.

"Okay then. We won't breathe a word of this to the matron," I said, zipping my mouth shut.

"Okay."

"Thanks for showing me the picture," I said, beaming at him.

"You're welcome, Laura."

"What do you do with this picture?" I asked, staring at the image of the naked man and the woman having sex.

"What do you mean?" Luca asked, narrowing his eyes.

"Why would you have this picture with you?" I asked, pointing at the pornographic picture.

"I use it for something...." Luca said, avoiding my gaze.

"For what?" I asked, looking clueless.

"I use it to touch myself," Luca whispered in my ear.

"Touch yourself?" I whispered back.

"Yeah."

"Don't we all touch ourselves from time to time?" I asked, rubbing my arms.

"That's not what it means," Luca said, ruffling his eyebrows.

"Then what does it mean?" I asked, impatiently.

"You wouldn't understand anyway," Luca said, dismissively.

"Oh, really? Try me," I said, folding my arms across my chest.

"Masturbation. Have you heard of it?" Luca asked, looking around the room nervously.

"No," I said, shaking my head like a toddler. "What does it mean?"

"It means nothing. I think we're done here," Luca said, his hand reaching for the doorknob on the bedroom door.

"What does masturbation mean, Luca?" I shouted at the top of my lungs.

"Could you say it any louder?" Luca hissed under his breath.

"I'll be quiet as a mouse. What does it mean?" I asked in a squeaky voice.

"I don't wish to rob your innocence any more than I already have," Luca said, looking away from me.

"My innocence? Why is everybody obsessed with the idea of innocence?" I said, scoffing.

"Because if you're not innocent as a child, you won't get into heaven," Luca said, stomping his feet in frustration.

"Does that mean you won't get into heaven?" I asked, pouting my lips.

"Probably not," Luca said with a heavy sigh.

"Why? I want you to come to heaven with me and Giulia," I said, taking his hands in mine.

"I know, but I have drowned in the sea of sin. It's too late to get out of it now," Luca said, shutting his eyes.

"We're all sinners, Luca. That's the fundamental belief behind Christianity. You're a sinner, so am I, so is Giulia, so is Reverend James and so is the matron, Miss Maria."

"Okay, I'll tell you what masturbation means, but don't tell of this to anyone," Luca said, placing a finger on his lips.

"I promise," I said, wrapping my pinky finger around his.

"To masturbate is to touch your genitals. When I masturbate, I touch my penis. When you masturbate, you touch your clit or your vagina."

"Eww! Why would anybody do that?" I asked, flinching.

"It's common to touch yourself when you're sexually aroused by someone or something."

"You're sexually aroused by this picture?" I asked, scrutinizing the picture.

"Don't you feel something when you look at this picture?" Luca asked, looking me straight in the eye.

"Yes.... I get dirty thoughts," I said with a coy smile.

"Those dirty thoughts lead you to touch yourself," Luca spoke in a very low voice.

"Can I touch myself?" I asked, twiddling my thumbs.

"You can, but you have to be discreet. Don't let anyone catch you doing it," Luca said, squeezing my arm.

"Is it something you're ashamed of?" I asked, my eyes widened.

"Yes. I feel guilty every time I touch myself," Luca said, hanging his head in shame.

"Then doesn't it mean it's a sin?" I asked with a puzzled expression.

"It's not a sin. We're made to feel guilty about it," Luca said, biting his bottom lip.

"I wasn't aware of that..." I said, staring into space.

"It's a perfectly normal and healthy thing to do," Luca said, taking a deep breath.

"Anyway, buck up. You're coming to heaven with me and Giulia, okay?" I said, giving him a pat on the back.

"Sure!" Luca said with a sparkle in his eyes.

Luca and I held each other's hands and walked out of my room. The matron was eyeing us to death. She never likes it when a boy and a girl talk to each other or hold each other's hands.

"No holding hands!" The matron barked at us.

"Okay, miss Maria," I said, taking my hand away from his.

"Praise be to the Lord," the matron said, drawing the sign of the cross in the air.

"Praise be," I said, bowing my head in front of her and making the sign of the cross.

"Praise be," Luca said, making the sign of the cross hastily.

We silently walked past the matron, but as soon as she was out of sight, we held hands again.

"Let's go to the chapel," I said, pointing in the direction of the old chapel.

"Okay," Luca said with a slight nod.

We dashed to the chapel on the count of three. We made a bet. The last person to reach the chapel would have to share the apple pudding we get for dinner with the one who wins the game for an entire week. I won the game, so Luca would have to share his apple pudding with me for the rest of the week.

"That's not fair," Luca said, groaning.

"You're a sore loser, Luca," I said, thumbing my nose.

When we entered the chapel, we saw Reverend James kneeling on the floor and reciting the Nicene Creed. We slowly slipped past him and sat in the front row. When he was done with his prayer, he got up and approached us with gentle footsteps. He was stealthy like a cat. His bare feet made no sound. We couldn't hear him when he came up behind us.

"Praise be to the Lord!" The pastor exclaimed as he gripped our shoulders,

"Praise be," Luca and I said in unison.

"What are you two doing here?" The pastor asked, gawking at us.

"We just came here to have a convo with the big man," I said, pointing up at the ceiling.

"Aren't you two goody two shoes?" The pastor asked, tousling our hair.

"I guess we are," Luca said with a nervous chuckle.

"Have you heard from Giulia?" The pastor asked, sounding concerned.

"No," I replied, shrugging,

"What about you, Luca?" The pastor asked, shifting his gaze from me to Luca.

"I haven't heard from her," Luca responded with a sad smile.

"If you hear from her, can you let me know?" The pastor asked, staring into my soul.

"Sure, Pastor James," I said as a chill ran down my spine.

"That girl was so pretty. She had the most beautiful smile. Her eyes lit up a room," The pastor said, dreamy-eyed.

"Yes, she IS lovely," Luca said, stressing the word "is."

"It would be tragic if something bad happened to her," the pastor said, resting his hands under his chin and shaking his head.

"Yes, it would. We'll let you know when Giulia gets in touch with us," I said, smiling at him.

"Thanks, dear," the pastor said, caressing my cheeks.

As soon as the pastor hobbled out of the chapel, Luca turned to me and grimaced.

"He has done something to her," Luca said, gritting his teeth.

"Why do you think that?" I asked, resting my hand on Luca's shoulder.

"Why does he refer to her in the past tense? She WAS so pretty. She HAD the most beautiful smile. Her eyes LIT up a room," Luca said, sounding tense.

"Yeah, I noticed that too. Strange...." I said with a grim expression.

I took Luca's sharp observation about the pastor into serious consideration.

CHAPTER TWO

THE WHITE ROSE

"A false witness will not go unpunished, and whoever pours out lies will perish." (Proverbs 19:9)

I was hellbent on confronting Pastor James, but Luca told me it would not be a wise move on my part. I was desperate to find answers, and I'd not found a single answer in the six months that she had disappeared. I need to know Giulia is alive and well.

"Luca, what if she's dead?" I asked, catching a sob in my throat.

"Don't say that, Laura. We're gonna find her no matter what. You hear me?" Luca said, holding my face in his hands.

We ambled to the children's home, taking in the scenic view around us. It was a long walk in the open grassland stretching from the chapel to the children's home. It was noon when we reached St. Agnes. We had beef noodle soup and cherry pie for lunch. During lunch, I asked Rudolfo, one of the boys in the children's home, if he had any information on the gardener who allegedly eloped with my sister.

"Information? I have loads of it?" Rudolfo said, shoving a piece of the pie into his piehole.

"Did the matron catch Giulia having sex with the gardener?" I asked inquisitively.

"No, she's bluffing. But there is reason to believe the gardener and Giulia are romantically involved with each other." Rudolfo said, gobbling down another piece of the pie as though his life depended on it.

"Really?" I asked, slowly moving away from him.

"Yes. One day, the matron went to the backyard to check on the flowers in the garden. She saw the gardener giving Giulia a white rose," Rudolfo said, slurping the beef noodle soup loudly.

"That doesn't mean they are in love with each other," Luca said with a vexed voice.

"Why would he give her a flower if he wasn't in love with her? A white rose, that too. Everyone knows the rose is a symbol of romance," Rudolfo said, putting his hands behind his head.

"Giulia loves white things. Be it white roses, white frocks, or white cats, and dogs," I said, smiling wistfully.

"Exactly. He knew she liked white roses, and he gave them to her because he loves her," Rudolfo said, clenching the wooden spoon.

"You make a fair point," I said, cracking my knuckles.

"Where does the gardener live?" Luca asked, getting up from his seat.

"He lives two blocks away from the children's home. There is a rusty green bicycle outside his house. You can't miss it," Rudolfo said as he licked the bowl clean.

"Thanks for the info, Rudolfo!" I said with a sunny smile.

"Anytime, Laura," Rudolfo said, flashing me a big grin.

We went to the gardener's house after lunch. We lied to the matron and told her we were going to the local park.

She was not too happy about it, but she let us go.

"What are you kids doing here?" The gardener asked, digging his index finger in his left ear.

"We came to see you. We're from St. Agnes children's home," I said with my hands behind my back like a timid schoolgirl.

"I know that. I've seen you two around," the gardener said, sizing us up.

"We came to ask you something," Luca said, briskly.

"Hey, aren't you Giulia's twin sister?" The gardener asked, gazing at me in wide-eyed wonder.

"Yes, and how do you remember her name so well?" I asked, narrowing my eyes.

"How can I not? She is the sweetest girl there. Always asked me how I was doing. God bless her soul," the gardener said, holding his hands on his chest.

"It's been more than six months since she went missing from the children's home," I said, folding my arms across my chest.

"What? What happened to poor sweet Giulia?" The gardener asked, looking alarmed.

"We don't know, but the matron told us you are in love with her. Is that true?" Luca asked, glaring at him.

"I love her, of course. I mean, who doesn't? But if you're asking me if I romantically love her, I don't. I'm not into kids. I ain't a pedophile," the gardener said, hurting.

"No one's accusing you of being a pedophile. We just wanna clear up the rumours," I said with a reassuring smile.

"And these rumours are coming from Miss Maria's filthy mouth, aren't they? She's a bitch!" The gardener said, spitting a glob of saliva on the ground out of spite.

"She told us she caught you having sex with Giulia in the garden," Luca said, eyeing him suspiciously.

"You cannot be serious right now! The matron has had it out for me since the start," the gardener said, grasping the ends of his hair.

"Did you do or say anything to give her the idea that you might be in love with Giulia?" I asked, looking him dead in the eye.

"I did give Giulia a white rose once, but that's because she loves white roses. She was a tad upset that day, so I wanted to cheer up the little kid. It wasn't a romantic gesture," the gardener said, huffing.

"Thanks for clearing that up," Luca said, clearing his throat.

"Anytime, kiddo. I bet the garden looks like a mess now that I'm no longer tending to it. I'll never get my job back," the gardener said with a doleful look on his face.

"Don't worry. The matron will come crawling to you on her knees when all the weed and grass overgrows in the garden. She's just worried her ego will be bruised if she asks you to come back and work at the children's home," I said, chuckling.

"That really made my day. I needed to hear that. Thanks, dear," the gardener said with a warm smile.

"We should get going now. See you soon at St. Agnes!" I said, waving at him.

"See you soon, kids!" The gardener said, waving back at us.

We reached the children's home at half past six in the evening. The matron was resting in her room. Thank God! We went to Luca's bedroom and shut the door quietly.

"So, the gardener is innocent," Luca said, taking a deep breath.

"He sure is," I said, deep in thought.

"The only suspect on our list now is Reverend James," Luca said, chewing his nails.

"Reverend James did not do anything to her," I said, shaking my head.

"Why do you say that?" Luca asked, stroking his chin.

"Pastor James may be a creep, but he's certainly not a killer," I said, sneering.

"I wouldn't put it past him. That man's got serial killer vibes," Luca said, shuddering.

"I say we go to his parsonage and snoop around for anything linking him with Giulia's disappearance," I said in a very low voice.

"I'm not on board with this idea of yours. It sounds terrible," Luca said, frowning.

"Well, if you wanna find Giulia, you gotta do whatever it takes," I said, jabbing him in the ribs.

"Okay, but if things go south, I'm ratting you out to the matron," Luca said, shaking his finger at me.

"Deal," I said, shaking his hand.

We had stale gruel and apples for dinner. It was awful! We waited till everyone went to bed before sneaking into the pastor's parsonage. Fortunately, the door was open, and he was nowhere to be seen.

Luca went to his study, and I went to his bedroom. Luca didn't find suspicious anything in his study. I found a bible and a rosary on his bedside table. But when I flipped through the pages of the Bible, a letter fell out of one of the pages of the Bible. I picked it up and gasped loudly.

"Luca, look what I found in his bedroom," I said, waving the letter in his face.

Luca rushed to the study, panting.

"What is it?" Luca asked, breathless.

My hands were trembling as I read the letter aloud.

"Dear Giulia,

I miss you, dear. Your piercing blue eyes, your lovely smile, your beautiful golden hair, your plump lips, your smooth skin, and your pure white frock. I miss all of you."

I'm praying to God for your safe return. Daddy is waiting for his little girl to come back home.

Love,

Rev. James"

"Gosh, this man is sick!" Luca said, grimacing.

"This letter proves he's innocent," I said with a disappointed look on my face.

"Doesn't this letter make him seem all the more guilty?" Luca asked, looking baffled.

"No, look carefully. He says in his letter that he is waiting for her to come back home. That means he thinks she's still alive," I said, running my finger along the last line in the letter.

"Oh yeah. That does prove he's innocent," Luca said, scratching the back of his neck.

Just as were about to leave the room, I noticed a Ziploc bag sticking out of a pillow on the bed. Luca went over to the bed and lifted the pillow. He was not ready for what he was about to see.

"What the hell? That is a little girl's underwear," Luca said, recoiling in disgust.

"That is Giulia's underwear!" I screamed, springing like a cat.

"What? How did he get his grimy hands on her underwear," Luca said, opening the Ziploc bag.

"I don't know," I said with a shrug.

"It has not been washed. It smells ripe," Luca said, sniffing the underwear and scrunching his nose.

"He has an underwear fetish," I said, gagging.

"He has done something horrible to her, Laura," Luca said, gripping my shoulders. "If he hasn't murdered her, then he must've abducted her."

"We need to keep an eye on this underwear thief," I said, gritting my teeth.

"We definitely should," Luca said with a somber expression.

"He's probably at the chapel now for the 9 o'clock prayer," I said, stuffing the underwear into the Ziploc bag.

"We need to leave now. He may come back any second," Luca said, grabbing the Ziploc bag.

"Let's go," I said, taking his hand in mine.

We darted outside the parsonage, not uttering a word. We stood outside the children's home, catching our breaths for what felt like forever.

"God, that was quite the adventure," Luca said, wheezing.

"We make a great team, don't we?" I said with a twinkle in my eye.

"We should become sleuths when we grow up. We're good at it," Luca said, grinning widely.

"Definitely," I said, grinning back at him.

"It's sad that the gardener was let go, and not the wretched pastor. The poor gardener didn't deserve it," Luca said, looking gloomy.

"È la vita," I said with a heavy sigh.

"I'm tired. I'm gonna hit the hay pretty soon," Luca said, stifling a yawn.

"Me too," I said with a weary smile.

I couldn't get a wink of sleep that night. My heart was pounding out of my chest. I tossed and turned in bed, wondering where Giulia was. A menacing voice echoed in my ears, *'She is dead.'*

CHAPTER THREE

Confronting the Underwear Thief

"Flee from sexual immorality. All other sins a person commits are outside the body, but whoever sins sexually, sins against their own body." (1 Corinthians 6:18)

I didn't have my breakfast the next day. I was too upset to eat anything. I wanted to know how Pastor James got my sister's underwear without her knowledge. I went to Luca's room after he had his breakfast.

"What did you have for breakfast?" I asked, my stomach growling with hunger.

"Chicken pot pie and grilled peaches," Luca said, licking his lips.

"That sounds scrumptious!" I said, rubbing my belly in circles.

"Why did you skip breakfast? You love chicken pot pie," Luca said, pouting.

"I do. It's just that I couldn't eat after everything that happened last night...." I said, shuddering.

"Oh yeah. That was horrifying, to say the least," Luca said, looking away from me.

"Where is her underwear?" I asked, looking around the room.

"It's here in the chest of drawers," Luca said, pointing at the chest of drawers.

"I'll take it with me," I said, heading to the chest of drawers.

"Sure. Please take it. I feel like a creep for holding onto her dirty underwear," Luca said, joining his hands together.

"No, you're not. Can't say the same for Pastor James, though," I said, picking up the Ziploc bag with the underwear in it.

"Yeah, about that. How did he get hold of her underwear?" Luca asked, frowning.

"He came to the children's home a few months ago. Giulia was too sick to attend mass. She had pneumonia. The Pastor said he'll give her the communion here. He must've taken it then."

"She just left her underwear lying around in her bed?" Luca asked, raising his eyebrows.

"No. He must've taken it from the pile of dirty clothes she keeps on her bedside table," I said, lost in thought.

"Maybe," Luca said with a shrug.

"He is a sicko!" I said, feeling sick to my stomach.

"No doubt about that," Luca said, looking unfocused.

"We need to rat him out to the matron," I said, clenching my teeth."Do you really think the matron's gonna take our side? For all we know, she's probably the one who gave him the underwear," Luca said, scorning.

"You really hate that woman, don't you?" I asked, grinning at him.

"Why wouldn't I hate her? She's a wolf in sheep's clothing," Luca said, taking a deep breath.

"So is Reverend James," I said, biting my bottom lip.

"I hope I don't run into Pastor James today," Luca said, brooding.

"Why would you? Are you going to the chapel later today?" I asked, narrowing my eyes.

"Yeah.... Just thought I'd sit there for a while. It's so serene in there," Luca said with a sigh.

"Please don't. You WILL run into him if you go to the chapel," I said, really hoping he wouldn't go to the chapel.

"Okay then. I won't go," Luca said, shaking his head like a toddler.

"On second thought, I think we should go to the chapel. We need to talk to him about the underwear," I said, stroking my chin.

"Most certainly not. Are you nuts?" Luca asked, scowling at me.

"Why? What's wrong?" I asked, sulking.

"You wanna ask him about her underwear? You don't think there's anything wrong with that," Luca said, looking me straight in the eye.

"We don't have any other choice, do we?" I said with a sad smile.

"When do we go?" Luca asked, glancing at his watch.

"After lunch. I heard we're having lamb chops and mashed potatoes," I said, gulping.

"God, I love lamb chops! We'll go after lunch.," Luca said with a twinkle in his eye.

"Reverend James, you better watch out for us," I said, balling my fists.

"I can't promise you I won't beat him black and blue if I see him," Luca said, cracking his knuckles.

"Please don't do that. We're just gonna ask him about the underwear. No fists, only words," I said, squeezing his arm.

"That sounds boring," Luca said, groaning.

"Giulia wouldn't want us to use our fists. She'd want us to have a rational conversation with him," I said, taking his hands in mine.

"What can I say? She's probably a pacifist," Luca said, scoffing.

"And I suppose you're not," I said, placing a hand on his shoulder.

"I just said I wanna beat him into a pulp. So, what do you think I am?" Luca asked, rolling his eyes.

"An aggressive and emo teen boy," I said, smirking.

"You're very honest, aren't you?" Luca said, shaking his finger at me.

"I call it like I see it," I said with a smug smile.

"You think the pastor has the matron's underwear?" Luca muttered under his breath.

"Can you imagine?" I said, giggling.

"No!"

"He hates her, so no, I don't think so," I said, shaking my head.

"You don't have to like someone to have their underwear," Luca said, scoffing.

"È vero, but the pastor clearly likes Giulia. You read that letter, didn't you?" I asked, stretching my arms.

"Yeah, her piercing blue eyes, soft skin, and plump lips. What a description!" Luca said, rubbing his temple.

"He refers to himself as 'daddy' and Giulia as his 'little girl,'" I said, gagging.

"Yuck! There's a special place in hell for people like him," Luca said, gritting his teeth.

"Definitely! If any other man did this, I wouldn't bat an eye, but he's a man of the cloth!" I said, looking upset.

"It's always the men of the cloth you've to be worried about," Luca said in a somber tone.

"Clearly. God help us all if there are more pastors like him out there in the big bad world," I said, raising my hands above my head.

We walked out of Luca's room to the corridor. The matron passed by us in the corridor.

"Praise be to the Lord," the matron said, sizing us up.

"Praise be," I said, lowering my gaze.

"Praise be," Luca said, sweating bullets.

"Laura, is that what I think it is?" The matron asked, taking a peek at the underwear in the Ziploc bag.

"Ummm....no," I said, hiding the Ziploc bag behind my back.

"Why are you holding your underwear in your hand?" The matron asked, folding her arms across her chest.

"No particular reason," I said, gulping hard.

"Is it not your underwear?" The matron asked, looking in Luca's direction.

"It is," I said, clearing my throat.

"Have you no shame holding your underwear when a boy is standing next to you?" The matron said, shifting her gaze from Luca to me.

"I honestly don't know what to say to that," I said with a blank look on my face.

"Were you fooling around with him without wearing your underwear?" The matron asked, eyeing me suspiciously.

"You mean if I had sex with him?" I asked, just to get under her skin.

"Don't you dare say that word!" The matron said, glaring at me.

"I didn't have sex with him," I said, deliberately repeating the word "sex" to make her mad.

"Are you wearing underwear right now?" The matron asked, looking below my waist.

"Yes," I said, pulling up my frock to show her my baby pink underwear.

"Then what in God's name are you doing with an extra pair of undies in your hand, Laura?" The matron asked, covering her face with his hands.

"I accidentally left it in Luca's bedroom, so I'm taking it back to my room," I said, gripping the Ziploc bag.

"You 'accidentally' dropped it in his bedroom," the matron said "accidentally" with air quotes.

"Yes. That's what I just said," I said, bluntly.

"Your mouth is full of lies, Laura," the matron said, pointing an accusing finger at me.

"No, it's not," I said, hurting.

"You will recite *Psalm 51* fifty-one times. Do you hear me?" The matron asked in a stern voice.

"Yes," I said with my hands behind my back.

"Now go to your room," the matron said, dismissively.

"Okay, Miss Maria," I said, sulking.

"And Luca, please go to your room. Don't tag along with her. She's a bad influence on you," the matron said, glaring at me.

"I'll go, Miss Maria. Have a blessed day," Luca said, sounding nervous.

"Have a blessed day, you two. Now scram," the matron said, raising her voice.

As soon as she left, we scurried to my room like rats.

"Phew! That was a close call," Luca said, wheezing.

"I know, right?" I said, catching my breath.

"She thinks we're having sex," Luca said, chuckling.

"Let her think what she thinks. I'm fine with her thinking we're doing the nasty," I said, smiling at him.

"Me too," Luca said, smiling back at me.

"She's just mad 'cause she's 40 and still a virgin," I said, sneering.

"She's a virgin?" Luca asked, his eyes nearly popping out of his sockets.

"Yes, she can't have sex. Why do you think she's so uptight?" I said, grouchily.

"Dio mio! It all makes sense now," Luca said, gasping softly.

After we had lunch, we left for the chapel. The pastor was praying by himself as usual.

"Praise be to the Lord," the pastor said, making the sign of the cross.

"Praise be," Luca said, closely watching him.

"Praise be," I said with a nervous smile.

"What are you kids doing here at his hour? Shouldn't you be having your lunch now?" The pastor asked, standing up.

"There's something I need to ask you," I said, standing right in front of him.

"What's it, dear?" The pastor asked, looking worried.

"Why do you have Giulia's underwear with you?" I asked, looking him dead in the eye.

"What are you saying, Laura?" The pastor asked, looking stunned.

"Don't play dumb, pastor. We know you stole her underwear," I said, balling my fists.

"You make me sound like an underwear thief," the pastor croaked.

"Didn't you steal it though?" I asked, narrowing my eyes.

"No, I didn't. Giulia gave it to me," the pastor said with a straight face.

"How stupid do you think we are? She wouldn't give it to me if I asked her, and I'm her twin!"

"I asked her to give me a pair of her undies, and she gave it to me." the pastor spoke in a very low voice.

"That's not possible. Nuh-huh.," Luca said, clicking his tongue.

"I told her all her sins would be absolved if she gave it to me," the pastor said with a half-smile.

"And she fell for it. How naïve of her!" I said, looking disappointed.

"I don't buy it for one second," Luca said, shaking his head.

"Believe it or not, that's what happened. I told her all her sins relating to lust would be absolved if she gave me her underwear."

"But she didn't lust after anyone," I said, my heart in my throat.

"She did. She confessed to me in the confession booth. She was lusting after you, Luca."

"What?"

"Yes, it's true. She told me she was having sinful thoughts about you. I told her to give me the underwear to absolve her sin of lust. It was meant to be symbolic."

"Why did she give you her used underwear?" I asked, staring daggers at him.

"I told her the underwear was sullied like her soul," the pastor said, moving towards me.

"We took the underwear from your study last night," Luca said, stepping between me and the pastor.

"When were you children in my parsonage?" The pastor said, looking alarmed.

"At night. When you were in the chapel for the 9 o'clock prayer," I said, chewing my upper lip.

"Oh, my Lord! You kids will be the death of me," the pastor said, clutching his chest.

"If you take one more girl's underwear, I'll report you to the matron," Luca said, shaking his finger at the pastor.

"Oh God, please don't. I despise that woman," the pastor said, hissing like a rattlesnake.

"Then don't take children's underwear like some pedophile," I said, stomping my feet in fury.

"Okay, I won't. I've to get going now," the pastor said, shuffling away from us.

The pastor did the walk of shame as he walked out of the chapel.

"Can you believe that guy?" I said, fuming.

"Certainly not," Luca said, shaking his head.

"We'll go now. It's getting dark," I said, looking outside the large casement in the chapel.

We reached the children's home in a matter of minutes. We straight went to my bedroom.

"What do we do with this guy?" I asked with my hands on my hips.

"I still think we should report him to the matron," Luca said, shifting his weight from one foot to the other.

"No, Luca. That's the stupidest thing I've ever heard from you," I said, scrunching up my face.

"What's to say he won't steal your underwear next?" Luca said, pointing his finger below my waist.

"Now that you put that thought in my mind, I really think he'll steal my underwear next," I said, holding my hands on my chest.

"Damn right, he will! Once an underwear thief, always an underwear thief," Luca said, grimacing.

"That's not a saying," I said, chuckling.

"I make it up as I go," Luca said, playfully nudging my arm.

"We're not ratting him out to the matron. Period!" I said, looking determined."If he steals your underwear, don't come crying to me," Luca said, wagging a finger in front of my face.

"Giulia probably reported him to the matron, and look where that got her," I said with a glum look on my face.

"You make a fair point," Luca said, ruffling his eyebrows.

"I always do. I'm gonna take a short nap. See you at dinner," I said, waving at him.

"See you then, Laura," waving back at me.

CHAPTER FOUR

THE GHOST OF GIULIA

"Look at my hands and my feet. It is I myself! Touch me and see; a ghost does not have flesh and bones, as you see I have." *(Luke 24:39)*

When I woke up at dawn, Giulia was standing beside my bed, peering at me like a little child. I couldn't believe my eyes. I spent more than six months searching for her, and there she was, just hanging out in my bedroom.

"Giulia, is that you?" I asked, aggressively rubbing my eyes.

She didn't respond. She just stood there, gazing at me with her piercing blue eyes.

"Giulia, please say something," I said with pleading eyes.

She looked away from me with a gloomy expression on her face and walked out of the room.

"Hey, where are you going?" I called out after her.

I chased after her to the corridor, but she vanished without a trace. I dashed to Luca's room and banged on his door.

"Luca, open the door. Luca!" I said, banging my fists against the door.

"What is it? Jeez! Can't you wait for like a second?" He asked, groaning.

"No, I can't," I said impatiently.

Luca opened the door a few seconds later. He looked like he wanted to slap me across the face.

"Whatever it is, can't it wait? Gosh, dang it!" Luca said, sounding cross.

"You're not gonna believe what I'm gonna say," I said, leaping in excitement.

"I can't believe you'd wake me up from my sleep like some kind of sadist," Luca said, sulking.

"You can kiss your sweet dreams goodbye. Are you ready for what I'm gonna tell you?" I asked, rubbing my hands together.

"No."

"I saw Giulia just now," I said, almost shouting.

"What? Where?" Luca asked, darting his eyes around the room.

"In my bedroom," I said with a big grin on my face.

"This is not the time for your sick jokes, Laura," Luca said, scowling at me.

"I'm not joking, Luca," I said, shaking my head.

"What, so she just appeared in your bedroom out of nowhere?" Luca said, scoffing.

"Exactly. She didn't utter a word to me," I said, looking upset.

"That's strange.... She goes missing for more than half a year and she doesn't say a word," Luca said, tapping his forefinger on his chin.

"I know, right? When I asked her to speak up, she ran out of the bedroom," I said with a sad smile.

"Where did she go?" Luca asked with a worried look on his face.

"I don't know. She just disappeared into thin air just like that," I said, making a "poof" sound.

"I have a hard time believing your story, Laura," Luca said, narrowing his eyes.

"I can't believe it myself," I said with a dumbfounded expression.

"You're sure this is not just one of your dreams that's so realistic that you mistake it for reality," Luca said, gazing into my eyes.

"No, it's not," I said, sounding annoyed.

"Let's look around the children's home. I'm sure we'll find her somewhere here," Luca said reassuringly.

Luca and I spent the next two hours searching every nook and cranny for her, but we couldn't find her anywhere.

"She's not here, Laura," Luca said, pouting.

"I swear I saw her just two minutes ago. She couldn't have gone that far. Am I going crazy?" I asked, blinking my eyes repeatedly.

"You might be. You're clearly having a hard time coping with her disappearance," Luca said, looking at me with pity.

"Are you seriously calling me crazy right now?" I asked, pointing an accusing finger at him.

"The mind processes grief in different ways. In your case, you're hallucinating about her," Luca said, slowly backing away from me.

"No, I'm not. I can prove it," I said, begging him.

"Really? How?" Luca asked, raising his eyebrows.

"Come with me to the chapel. I'm sure she's there. She always loved going to the chapel," I said, tugging at his arm.

"I don't wanna see that underwear thief again. I might knock his lights out," Luca said, balling his fists.

"He won't be there now. He's usually having breakfast at the parsonage at this hour," I said, chewing my nails.

"Whatever you say. You better be right, missy," Luca said, shaking his finger at me.

"I'm a hundred percent right, mister," I said, squeezing his arm.

We went to the chapel after breakfast. As I had predicted, Pastor James wasn't there.

"What did I tell you, Luca? Didn't I tell you he wouldn't be here at this hour of the day?" I said in a teasing tone.

"Okay, great. You want a trophy for guessing right?" Luca asked, rolling his eyes.

"Don't be a jerk, Luca," I said, huffing.

"I'm a jerk? You're the biggest jerk for waking me up when the ghosts are still out and about," Luca said, stomping his feet.

"Stop being such a whining baby. It doesn't suit you," I said, sticking my tongue out.

"Okay, so where is she?" Luca asked with a blank look on his face.

"Just wait a minute, Luca. She'll turn up any second now," I said, really hoping she'd turn up.

Seconds became minutes; minutes became an hour. She still didn't turn up.

"I can't believe I let you talk me into coming here. What a waste of time!" Luca said, throwing his hands up in the air.

"Luca, I swear I saw her in my bedroom. Why don't you believe me when I say I saw her?" I said, hurting.

"Laura, I hate saying this, but your grief is making you act out of sorts. Just get some rest. You'll be alright," Luca said, tousling my hair.

"For the last time, it wasn't a hallucination," I said, getting frustrated.

"There where the heck is she, Laura? Where is she? Show me," Luca said, folding his arms across his chest.

"Just give it some time," I said, dreading she wouldn't show up.

"I've spared enough time of my day entertaining your madness. I'm leaving now. I'm sorry," Luca said, walking away from me.

"Go on then. Don't ever talk to me, Luca. You've never truly loved Giulia. If you did, you wouldn't act the way you're acting right now. And to think she lusted after you," I said, glaring at him.

"I love her, Laura. Your head is so far up your butt to notice that," Luca said, fuming.

"Luca, stop talking," I said, shushing him.

"You can't tell me when to stop talking. I can't talk whenever I want," Luca grumbled.

"Luca, seriously shut up. Giulia is here," I said, moving closer to her.

"Where?" Luca asked, scratching his head.

"In front of us," I said, holding out my hand. Giulia took my hand in hers.

"I don't see her," Luca said, looking lost.

"Look, she's there. Right in front of your eyes," I said, pointing my forefinger in Giulia's face.

"No one's there, dummy," Luca said, knocking me on the head.

"She's looking at us, Luca. She's wearing her favourite white frock," I said, smiling at her.

"I don't see her, Laura. You're seeing things," Luca said, ruffling his eyebrows.

"I really am losing my marbles," I said, shutting my eyes.

"It's okay. It happens," Luca said, placing a hand on my shoulder.

''I need to leave now," I said, tears stinging my eyes.

I ran out of the chapel, weeping bitterly. Luca came running after me.

"Laura, where are you going?" Luca said, grabbing my arm.

"Stay away from me, Luca. I'm crazy," I said, struggling to get my arm out of his viselike grip.

"Aren't we all a little crazy?" Luca said, lacing his fingers through mine

"Not like this. I'm batshit crazy," I said, wiping my tears with the back of my hand.

"No, you're not. Come back," Luca said, pulling me closer to him.

"Leave me alone," I said, squirming.

"You're her twin, Laura. You would be crazy if you didn't hallucinate about her," Luca said, brushing aside a long strand of golden hair from my face.

"You're not helping, Luca," I said, covering my face with my hands.

"Laura, I didn't mean what I said back at the chapel. I admit I'm a jerk," Luca said, caressing my cheeks.

"You're not a jerk. Who would wake someone up in the middle of their sleep?" I said, looking sullen.

"You're worried about your twin, and I'm worried about my beauty sleep. I'm a jerk," Luca said, looking away from me.

"Luca..."

"In this time of grief, I should be there for you, Laura. Not snoozing in my bed."

"I can't stay mad at you," I said, grinning at him.

"Thank God for that! Let's get some fuel in your system," Luca said, tickling my stomach.

"Luca, stop!" I said, giggling.

"No, I won't," he said as he continued to tickle me.

"Seriously, stop it! I'll die of laughter," I said, doubling over with laughter.

"Isn't that the best way to die?" Luca asked with a chuckle.

"It is!" I said with a slight nod of the head.

"I'll tickle you to death then," Luca said, wiggling his fingers.

"You truly love Giulia, don't you?" I asked, elbowing him.

"I fell in love with her the moment I first laid my eyes on her," Luca said, dreamy-eyed.

"Oh my God! Really?" I squealed with delight.

"I told myself it was my future wife who was standing in front of me," Luca said with a coy smile.

"That's so sweet! I'll find your future wife even if it kills me," I said, lifting his chin.

"We'll find her together," Luca said, taking my hands in his.

"She'd be so lucky to be with a guy like you," I said, smiling wistfully.

"You'll find a nice guy too," Luca said, squeezing my shoulder.

"I don't know about that. Jerks always attract jerks, don't they?" I said with a heavy sigh.

"Again, you're not a jerk, Laura. Besides, don't you know that saying; opposites attract each other? So, if you're a jerk, you'll attract someone who's anything but a jerk."

"You're right. I'll find a nice guy," I said, blushing.

"If things go south for you, I'll marry both you and Giulia. You and Giulia shared the same womb, and you'll be sharing the same husband. No biggie."

"I'm actually not opposed to that idea. But we are Christians, dummy. You can't have more than one wife."

"I was just kidding, Laura. I'm not gonna marry you. One wife is more than I can handle," Luca said, smirking.

"Oh, you think I don't know that? I was just playing along with your stupid idea," I said, nudging his arm.

"Oh yeah?" He looked at me flirtatiously. I got butterflies in my stomach. I'd never felt that way before.

Luca lifted me in his arms and whizzed past the open grasslands.

"Put me down this instant, Luca," I said as my soft bouncy boobs pressed against his rock-hard chest.

I turned to my left and saw Giulia looking at me. I could say she was hurting. I felt a sharp pang of guilt in my chest.

"Luca, please put me down," I said, gazing into his honey-brown eyes.

"I won't," Luca said, looking at me with tender affection.

"I really mean it. Put me down now!" I said, banging my fists against his chest.

"Okay, jeez! I was just having some jolly good fun with you," Luca said, lowering me to the ground gently.

"How can you carry me around in your arms when Giulia is still missing?" I said, biting my bottom lip.

"You make me sound like I'm cheating on her with you," Luca said, his eyes widened.

"You are, Luca!" I said, tears welling up in my eyes.

"I don't love you, Laura. My heart belongs to Giulia. Don't get any ideas," Luca said, holding up the palm of his hand.

My heart shattered into a million little pieces like tiny shards of glass when he said that. I didn't love him, but I felt his words cut through me like a knife. We resumed the rest of the journey in complete silence. We ate our lunch about an hour later and never once exchanged glances. Things got awkward between us real quick.

THE BLOOD-SOAKED WHITE FROCK

"Who knows if the human spirit rises upward and if the spirit of the animal goes down into the earth?" (Ecclesiastes 3:21)

I didn't speak a word to him after that incident. He really hurt my feelings. I know that he loves my twin sister, but he doesn't have to rub it in my face. I'm only human. I was taking a walk in the open grassland when I saw her again.

"Giulia, are you headed to the chapel?"

She nodded her head and moved closer to me.

"I'm going there too. Let's go too."

I tried to take her hand in mine, but I couldn't feel her hand. My hand just went through hers.

"Giulia, you're not real?"

She stared at me but didn't say anything.

"Are you a ghost?"

There was still no response from her. I tried touching her face and her arms, but I was just touching air.

"What happened to you, Giulia?"

She looked at me, tears streaming down her face.

"Did someone hurt you?"

Giulia gave a slight nod.

"Who was it? Who hurt you?"

She looked at the chapel in the distance and heaved a sigh.

"Was it Reverend James?"

She had a blank look on her face.

"Did Pastor James hurt you?"

She pointed her forefinger at St. Agnes.

"Was it Miss Maria?"

She shook her head, looking disappointed.

"Was it the gardener?"

She pouted her lips and shook her head vigorously.

"Who was it, Giulia?"

I noticed a huge red stain below the waist of her white frock.

"What is that?"

I tried rubbing the blood stain with my hands, but it wasn't going. It was an old stain.

"How did you get this?"

She turned away from me and started sobbing.

"Giulia, I didn't mean to make you cry. I'm sorry......"

She squeezed my shoulder. Her eyes told me everything was going to be okay.

"I'll find the person who hurt you."

She smiled at me and walked into the chapel. When I entered the chapel, she wasn't there. I got on my knees and prayed to God for three hours straight and went to the children's home in time for dinner.

"Why are you not eating anything, Laura?" Rudolfo said, staring at my bowl of carbonara pasta.

"I don't feel hungry," I said, but I was obviously lying. I was so hungry I could've eaten a horse.

"But you like carbonara pasta, don't you?" Rudolfo asked, pouting.

"I do. I just don't want to eat anything. I wanna throw up," I said, gagging.

"You might be sick. Just drink this Minestrone and go to bed," Rudolfo said, smiling at me.

"That's the plan," I said with a half-smile.

I went to my room and got in my bed, weeping. My biggest fear had finally come to pass.

"Laura, are you alright?" Luca asked, peeking his head into the bedroom.

"Yes...."

"I saw you didn't eat dinner. You just had the Minestrone. Just wanted to check up on you," Luca said, closing the bedroom door gently.

"That's so thoughtful of you," I said, sniveling. "I'm supposed to be mad at you, but I can't. You're too sweet,"

"I'm really sorry for what I said earlier. I love you, Laura. I care about you," Luca said, squeezing my arm.

"I know, but that's on me for assuming you were flirting with me," I said, cringing.

"I might've crossed a line there. I shouldn't have lifted you in my arms. That was not okay," Luca said, looking away from me.

"It's okay. That's all water under the bridge at this point," I said, holding out my hand.

"Yeah, let's bury the hatchet," Luca said, firmly shaking my hand.

"She's dead, Luca," I said, tears stinging my eyes.

"Who?"

"Giulia...." I said, blubbering.

"No, she's not. Why would you say that?" Luca asked, looking upset.

"I saw her again," I said, taking a deep breath.

"Not this again. Laura...." Luca said, rubbing his temple.

"And she isn't real, Luca; she's a ghost," I said in a hollow voice.

"How do you know that, Laura?" Luca asked doubtfully.

"I couldn't feel her hand. I couldn't feel any part of her body," I said, swaying my arms.

"But how sure are you that she's dead?" Luca asked, really hoping she wasn't dead.

"I hadn't noticed this before, but she had a blood stain on her frock. It was near her you-know-where," I said, pointing my index finger between my legs.

"In her nether region," Luca said, raising his eyebrows.

"Yes."

"That can only mean one thing," Luca said, shaking me by the shoulders.

"What?"

"She was sexually assaulted," Luca said with an exasperated sigh.

"Huh?"

"She was raped, Laura," Luca said, dread written all over his face.

"I don't understand. What is 'rape'?" I asked, blankly.

"It is non-consensual sex. Someone has forcefully had sex with her, hence the blood stain in the nether region," Luca said, breathing heavily.

"That cannot be true," I said, shaking my head.

"It is."

"Why didn't she tell me she was raped?" I asked, hurting.

"Maybe because she was killed when she was getting raped," Luca said, deep in thought.

"That's horrible! Don't say that," I said, flinching.

"Do you think it was Reverend James?" Luca asked with all the curiosity of a cat.

"Unfortunately, it's not him," I said, looking disappointed.

"How do you know it wasn't him?" Luca asked, narrowing his eyes.

"When I asked Giulia, she shook her head," I said, looking down at the floor.

"Who is it then?" Luca asked with a puzzled expression.

"She pointed at the children's home when I asked her who hurt her," I said, scratching my nose.

"So, it's someone from here. Is it the matron?" Luca asked in a hoarse whisper.

"No, it wasn't her. When I told her it was the matron, she disagreed with me," I said, chewing her upper lip.

"Then who else can it be?" Luca asked, losing his patience. "It could be one of the guys here."

"You're saying one of the boys here raped her? How can they rape her when they don't even know what it means?" I asked, shifting my weight from one foot to the other.

"You don't need to know the meaning of rape to rape someone," Luca said, looking surprised.

"Yeah, you're right. I'm dumb," I said, feeling embarrassed.

"You're not dumb. You're just overwhelmed by what you saw," Luca said, placing a hand on my shoulder.

"I don't think the boys here are capable of hurting a fly," I said, plopping down on the bed.

"You couldn't have been more wrong," Luca said, sitting beside me in bed.

"No way."

"I once heard Marco tortured a kitten. He strangled it till it was blue in the face. After he killed the kitten, he tossed it in a gunny bag and threw it in the dump yard."

"Really?" I asked, jumping up from the bed.

"Yeah, there was a rotten smell in the dump yard for weeks after that," Luca said, wrinkling his nose.

"What happened to its mother?" I asked, my voice cracking.

"It was desperately searching for the kitten. It died a day later of unbearable grief," Luca said with a gloomy face.

"Oh, poor cat!" I exclaimed, putting my hand on my chest. "What about the other kittens?"

"They're getting by without their mom. They won't last long," Luca said, looking devastated.

"We need to bring them here, Luca," I said, turning to face him.

"Are you crazy? The matron will murder you," Luca spoke through clenched teeth.

"I don't care! We need to save their souls," I said, pacing about the room anxiously.

"'Cats don't have souls.' That's what the matron said," Luca said, looking unfocused.

"What rubbish! Won't they go to heaven after they die?" I asked with puppy-dog eyes.

"According to Miss Maria, 'Only humans have souls and only we can enter heaven,'" Luca said, scorning.

"I'm sure there's cat heaven somewhere up there," I said with a sullen look on my face.

"Hopefully," Luca said, making the sign of the cross.

"We need to get them before they die," I said, my breath shuddering.

"I guess we could sneak them into your bedroom after everyone has fallen asleep," Luca said, stroking his chin.

"That's a good idea. Let's do that," I said, snapping my fingers.

We went to the backyard after everyone retreated to their rooms for the night. It was a full moon night.

"Where are the kitties?" I asked, looking around the backyard.

"They're in the garden," Luca said, pointing towards the garden.

When we crept to the garden, we saw Marco waving a knife in front of the kittens. The kittens scurried away from him and meowed.

"What are you doing, Marco?" I asked, folding my arms across my chest.

"Come to papa, so you can meet your mama tonight. Sweet dreams," Marco said, leering.

"I said, what are you doing, Marco?" I asked, raising my voice.

"What do you think I'm doing? I'm killing them," Marco said, tsking.

"The hell you will," I said, gritting my teeth.

I grabbed the knife from Marco and slashed his thighs. Blood pooled in his pants.

"Puttana! You'll pay for this," Marco said, wincing.

"If you so much as harm a hair on her head, I'll butcher you with this knife," Luca said, taking the knife from me and pointing it in Marco's face.

"Why are you siding with this cagna?" Marco asked, howling in pain.

"Don't you dare call her a cagna! The only cagna here is you," Luca said, spitting on the ground.

"Let me get the job done in peace. Don't stick your nose where it doesn't belong," Marco said, clenching his teeth.

"If you kill the kittens, we'll kill you," I said, raising my fist to punch him in the face.

"I can't tell if you're joking or if you're serious right now?" Marco said, chortling.

"Does it look like we're joking?" Luca said, scowling at him.

"Why would you harm these poor creatures? They can't even speak for themselves," I said, catching a sob in my throat.

"I enjoy killing kittens. I killed their mom. Might as well kill them too. End their pain once and for all," Marco said, laughing uproariously.

"Children who kill animals grow up to become serial killers," Luca said, grimacing.

"That is not real," Marco said, scoffing.

"Today, you stuff a cat's carcass in a gunny bag. Tomorrow, you'll stuff a cadaver in a gunny bag," Luca said, looking him dead in the eye.

"Whatever," Marco said, rolling his eyes.

He left the kittens alone and limped his way to the children's home. As soon as he left, I took a tabby in my arms and caressed it. Its eyes were glowing in the dark.

"It's scared to death. The poor thing," I said, stroking its little head.

"Let's take them to their new home," Luca said, booping the tabby's nose.

I carried the tabby and the white kitty in my arms. Luca took the black and grey one. When we reached the children's home, the cats started mewling loudly.

"I think they're hungry. They're used to drinking their mother's milk. They're too young to have solid foods," I said, sounding worried.

"Just go to your room. I'll come back," Luca said, handing me the black and the grey cat.

Luca tiptoed into the kitchen, stole a jug of warm milk from the fridge and a wooden bowl from the counter, and brought them to my room. No sooner had Luca poured the milk into the bowl than the cats slurped it up in one sip.

"They really loved it!" I said, cradling the white cat in my arms.

"I'm glad they loved it. They'll sleep safe tonight, thanks to us. I'll leave you to them. Sleep tight, Laura!" Luca said, kissing the black cat's furry head. It purred softly.

"Goodnight, Luca," I said, waving him goodbye.

I cuddled the kittens in bed and soon fell asleep. It felt so good to be a mother of four kittens, even if it was just for one night.

CHAPTER SIX

THE PRICE OF SELF-RESTRAINT

"Like a city whose walls are broken through is a person who lacks self-control." (Proverbs 25:28)

I was playing with the kittens in the morning when the door swung wide open.

"Laura, how dare you bring the kittens in here!" The matron yelled at me.

"They were gonna die. They just lost their mother, so I'm looking after them for now," I said, holding the grey cat close to my chest.

"You need to get a good whooping, or you won't learn your lesson," the matron said, incensed.

Luca heard the matron yelling and came rushing to the room.

"What is happening here?" Luca asked, shifting his gaze from the matron to me.

"Your little girlfriend brought these kittens here without my permission, and I'm giving her a piece of my mind. That's what's happening," the matron said, glaring at me.

"I was part of this too. I helped her bring the kittens here," Luca said, moving closer to me.

"I'm very disappointed in you, Luca. Didn't I tell you she's a bad influence on you?" The matron said, shaking her head.

"Please don't hit her. Hit me instead. I'll take all the whoopings," Luca said, lowering his head.

"Aren't you a little Jesus?" The matron said with a menacing smile.

"She's already grieving the loss of her sister. She's not herself right now," Luca said, looking at me with sympathy.

"Both the sisters are out of control. One runs away with the gardener and the other sneaks the kittens in here when she knows full well she shouldn't," the matron said, snarling.

"One's not like the other, Miss Maria," Luca said, looking away from me.

"Leave the room now, Luca. Take the kittens and go," the matron said dismissively.

Luca obeyed her, took the kittens, and left the room. As soon as he left the room, she shut the door.

"You're gonna regret what you did," the matron said, turning to face me.

She pulled out a leather belt from one of her crimson-coloured sleeves and started whipping me with it.

"You're hurting me. Stop!" I screamed in agony.

"You don't mess with me and get away with it," the matron said as she continued to whip me brutally.

Luca heard the whipping sound and started banging on the door.

"Miss Maria, stop whipping her this instant. If you don't stop now, I'll break open this door," Luca said, banging his fists against the door.

"Go ahead. Break open the door," the matron said as she repeatedly whipped me.

Luca tried breaking the door open, but it was made of sturdy wood. He finally gave up. He took the kittens to the garden, left them there, and came running back to the children's home.

"Remove your frock," the matron ordered me.

"No," I said, stubbornly shaking my head like a toddler.

"Do it now!" The matron barked at me.

I removed my white frock and dropped it to the floor. I was standing in my petticoat.

"I have to go harder on you, or you'll repeat the same mistakes," the matron said, stretching her arms.

She thrashed me for the next fifteen minutes. My back was bleeding profusely. I couldn't feel the pain anymore. I was numb to it. After she was done with me, she tucked the belt into her sleeve and stormed out of the room.

"Laura, are you okay?" Luca said, rushing towards me.

I didn't say anything. I just stood there, staring at him.

"Please say something," Luca said, taking my trembling hands in his.

I just walked out of the room wearing nothing but my petticoat.

"Where are you going?" Luca asked, following me like a puppy.

"Leave me alone!" I said, wiping my tears with the back of my hand.

I ran outside the children's home and went to the chapel. It was the only place I could seek solace. I was dying to speak to my twin sister. I knew she'd be there waiting for me. I didn't eat my breakfast or lunch. It was more than three hours since I left the children's home. Lunch was served at twelve on the dot. Luca didn't touch a morsel of his food.

"Luca, eat something," Gianna, one of the girls in the children's home, said with a concerned look.

"No, I can't. I need to know where Laura went," Luca said, getting up from his seat.

Luca got up and dashed to the chapel, but I wasn't there.

"Where are you, Laura? Say something," Luca said, cupping his mouth with his hands.

He looked around the chapel for another few minutes. Then he left the chapel and walked towards the open grassland. He saw a mound in the distance and ran towards it.

"Laura, here you are. I was looking everywhere for you," Luca said, panting.

I just lay there as still as a corpse.

"Laura, get up. God, dang it!" Luca said, kneeling by my side.

He lifted me in his arms and carried me to the children's home.

"I saw Giulia.... She was here with me till you came here," I mumbled.

"I told myself I'd never carry you in my arms again. Yet I'm here doing just that," Luca said, gazing into my hazel eyes.

"Maybe it's fate. Who knows?" I said, groaning. I was losing a lot of blood.

Just as he was heading to the children's home, Pastor James came running towards us.

"What's going on, kids?" The pastor asked, holding up his black robe.

"Miss Maria whipped Laura for sneaking some kittens into her room without her permission," Luca said, tapping my cheeks lightly to make sure I was still conscious.

"This is exactly why I hate her. Who hits children?" The pastor said, clicking his tongue

"You're no better. She beats children. You just molest them," Luca said, sneering.

"Why didn't you come to me? Did you know I studied medicine before turning to priesthood?" Pastor James said with gleaming eyes.

"What happened then?" Luca asked, seeming uninterested.

"I flunked out of medical school," the pastor said, looking dejected.

"It figures," Luca said, rolling his eyes.

"I may not know much, but I certainly know enough to treat her," the pastor said, holding my hands.

"We'll ask the matron to bring in a certified doctor to treat her," Luca said, sounding annoyed.

"You think she'll do that? She whipped her to death. She'd want her to bleed to death," the pastor said with a doleful expression.

"Okay, you can treat her, but I'll be in the room the entire time," Luca said, narrowing his eyes.

"Why?" The pastor asked, looking muddled.

"What if you steal her underwear while tending to her wounds? She's semi-conscious. She wouldn't know if you took it," Luca said, sounding cross.

"Very funny. You can be there with me," the pastor said with a chuckle.

Luca carried me to the parsonage. The pastor asked Luca to take me to his bedroom. Luca gently laid me in bed.

"Okay, let's begin. Bring me two ice packs and the ointment over there," the pastor said, beckoning him to go to the sitting room.

Luca left the room to go get the ice packs and the ointment. After he left, the pastor started undressing me.

"Okay, let's get you out of this blood-stained petticoat," the pastor said, pulling the petticoat over my head.

Luca came in holding the tube of ointment in one hand and the two ice packs in the other.

"Look at those wounds. It looks like the branches of a tree," the pastor said, gasping softly.

"She's bleeding to death, and you're bothered about the shape of her wounds?" Luca said, scowling at him.

"Yeah, right. Sorry. Hand me the ice packs," the pastor said, holding out his hand.

He placed the ice packs on my gashes. Luca couldn't bear to look at the fresh wounds on my back.

"She'll be fit as a fiddle by tomorrow," the pastor said, stroking my hair gently.

The pastor slowly unhooked my bra and tossed it to the side of the bed. Luca's face turned red as a tomato.

"Is it necessary to remove her bra?" Luca asked with a nervous chuckle.

"Yes. The underwire in her bra is cutting into her skin," the pastor said, closely inspecting her wounds.

"Oh, okay. I see," Luca said, stroking his chin.

I suddenly turned to the other side, and Luca caught a glimpse of my bare breasts.

"I need to go to the bathroom. Do you have a bathroom?" Luca asked, covering his nether region with his hands.

"Of course, where else would I shower, poop and pee?" The pastor asked, looking surprised.

He pointed to the bathroom beside the almirah. Luca darted to the bathroom and shut the door.

"Oh shit! I'm a terrible human being," Luca said, resting his hands above his head.

Luca got a massive boner, and he pressed it tightly to get rid of the boner, but it was in vain.

"Why do you have to come now?" Luca whined. "This can't be happening now. I'm worse than the pastor."

It took immense self-control to not beat his meat. He got blue balls as a result. It hurt like hell. He came out of the bathroom several minutes later.

"What were you doing in there?" The pastor asked, looking in Luca's direction.

"Oh, nothing. Just taking a huge dump," Luca said, ruffling his hair.

"Hope you didn't stink up the place," the pastor said with a hearty laugh.

"Are you done treating her?" Luca asked, closing the bathroom door.

"Yeah, you can take her," the pastor said, smiling at me.

Luca lifted me in his arms and carried me to the children's home. On the way there, he gazed into my eyes. I was half awake now.

"I need to tell you something, Laura. Please don't get mad at me," Luca said, sounding nervous.

"What's it?" I asked, blinking my eyes.

"You know how I said I get sexually aroused by that picture," Luca said, his voice cracking.

"You mean the picture of that naked man and woman?" I asked, raising my eyebrows.

"Yes. Today's the first time I got sexually aroused by a real human being and not a picture," Luca said with a heavy sigh.

"Who is it?" I asked, wondering who this person was.

"You!" Luca cried.

"What do you mean?" I asked, looking clueless.

"The pastor removed your bra to apply some ointment and place the ice packs on your back. You turned to the other side, and I saw your twins," Luca said, cupping his chest with both his hands.

"Oh, really?" I asked, feeling embarrassed.

"Yes. I pitched a huge tent," Luca said, biting his bottom lip.

"Pitched a tent?" I asked, wondering how he could've pitched a tent in the parsonage.

"I got a boner because of your breasts," Luca said, gawking at my breasts out of the corner of his eye.

"What is a boner?" I asked, thinking he was actually referring to a bone.

"I swear to God, you're so naïve, Laura!" Luca said, sounding exasperated.

"Sorry..." I said, pouting my lips.

"Boner is when your penis becomes erect because you're sexually aroused by someone or something. The only way to get rid of it is to masturbate or have sex," Luca said, exhaling slowly.

"Did you masturbate?" I asked, looking him straight in the eye.

"No, I didn't. I should've, but I didn't. I got blue balls," Luca said, wincing.

"What's that?" I asked, annoyed that he was throwing all these new terms at me.

"When you don't satisfy your sexual needs, you get blue balls. It's extremely painful," Luca said, averting his gaze.

"I'm sorry, Luca...." I said, feeling bad for him.

"I'm limping right now as I speak," Luca said with a sad smile.

"I don't blame you. Your body wants what it wants, yet you refrained from masturbating. It mustn't have been easy," I said, caressing his soft cheeks.

"It felt wrong to touch myself when you were bleeding to death there," Luca said, moping.

"I wasn't bleeding to death. Stop exaggerating," I said, scoffing.

"Did you see your wounds? The pastor described them as 'the branches of a tree,'" Luca said, smiling wistfully.

"I can't believe you took me to the underwear thief after everything that happened," I said, visibly upset.

"What could I do? The matron wouldn't bring in a doctor, and the pastor was willing to help," Luca said, sulking.

"Thanks anyway," I said, smiling at him.

Luca carried me to my room and gently laid me in bed.

"Take care, Laura. Sweet dreams," Luca said softly, kissing me on the forehead.

"Sweet dreams, Luca," I said, blowing him a kiss.

Luca went to his room and got on his knees. He looked at the crucifix hanging over his bed and cried.

"Don't tempt me, Lord," Luca said, joining his hands in prayer.

He limped to the bathroom, removed his boxers, and peered down at his pene.

"Oh, God. It's swollen," Luca said, looking startled.

He touched it and winced in pain.

"The price of self-restraint," Luca said, heaving a sigh.

He washed his hands in the sink with crumbling blue soap, staggered out of the bathroom and got in bed, whimpering. He dreamt of me all night long.

CHAPTER SEVEN

FALLING FOR LUCA

"Whoever does not love does not know God, because God is love." (1 John 4:8)

My back was still sore from all the thrashings I got the day before. I woke up, slowly clutching my back. Just then, there was a gentle knock on my bedroom door.

"Who is it?" I asked, stifling a yawn.

"The matron," Luca said in a gruff voice.

"Haha. Very funny," I said, smirking.

Luca opened the door, grinning from ear to ear.

"Someone slept well last night," I said, nudging his arm.

"Yeah, I did. I had a wonderful dream," Luca said with a bashful smile.

"What did you dream about?" I asked eagerly.

"More like whom I dreamt about," Luca corrected me.

"Who did you dream about?"

"Umm.... Giulia. I dreamt of our wedding day." Luca said with a coy smile.

"Aww! I'm gonna tear up," I said, tears welling up in my eyes.

"Please don't," Luca said, sounding worried.

"How's your little guy there doing?" I asked, eyeing below his waist.

"Little guy?" Luca asked, looking confused.

"Your penis," I said, brushing my hand against his crotch.

"He's doing alright. He hurt me so bad last night, but he's cool with me now," Luca said with a sunny smile.

"That's great," I said, tousling his hair.

"So, what do you wanna do today?" Luca asked, cracking his knuckles.

"I'll just have my breakfast and go to the chapel," I said, stretching my legs.

"Nooo! Haven't you seen enough of that underwear thief?" Luca moaned.

"He may be a perv, but he saved my life," I said, holding my hands on my chest.

"He didn't save your life. I did. If it weren't for me, you'd still be lying outside the chapel bleeding to death," Luca said, sounding offended.

"I can't thank you enough for that," I said, taking his hands in mine.

"If you wanna find a way to thank me, come out to the garden and play with me," Luca said with pleading eyes.

"You know I can't, Luca. I need to speak to my sister," I said, looking away from him.

"Why doesn't Giulia wanna speak with me?" Luca said, looking dejected.

"She will. Just give her some time," I said, resting my head on his shoulder.

Luca tagged along with me to the chapel after breakfast. As usual, the pastor was there on his knees praying.

"Not this guy again...." Luca said, rubbing his temple.

"Praise be to the Lord," the pastor said, making the sign of the cross.

"Praise be," I said, making the sign of the cross quickly.

"Praise be," Luca said, making the sign of the cross in annoyance.

"The number of times we've run into you these past few days...." Luca said, scowling at him.

"It's what the Lord wants for us," the pastor said, raising his hands in the air.

"Did you ever want to become a priest? Or did you just choose priesthood as a last resort after flunking out of medical school?" Luca asked, giving him the stink eye.

"I've wanted to become a priest ever since I was a child. That was always my second option."

"Guess God didn't want you to go into the medical field," I said, chewing my upper lip.

"I guess not."

"Sorry if I sound like I'm crossing a line, but have you ever had a girlfriend?" Luca asked, folding his arms across his chest.

"Yes."

"Was she a little girl?" Luca asked, sneering.

"No! I'm not a pedofilo," the pastor said, hurting.

"No, no, you're not a pedofilo. You're just a man who steals little girls' mutandine," Luca said, glaring at him.

"I fell prey to the desires of my flesh. It was a moment of weakness, but I've vowed to the Lord I'll never do it again."

"You better not do it again!" I said, scoffing.

"As I was saying, yes, I had a girlfriend. She was actually a few years older than I was," the pastor said, taking a deep breath.

"How ironic!" Luca said, snickering.

"I was seventeen and she was twenty. She left me for another guy when I flunked out of medical school. I felt like I was good for nothing...."

"So sorry to hear that," I said in a pitiful tone.

"That guy became a doctor. She didn't though. She got knocked up before she graduated from medical school."

"They got married, right?" Luca asked, raising his eyebrows.

"Yeah. She has been married to him for more than five years now and she has a son," the pastor said, tears fighting back tears.

"Did you ever see her after you flunked out of medical school?" I asked, looking gloomy.

"Yes. She's a member of the church I served in before I was sent here," the pastor said as tears spilled down his translucent cheeks.

"Oh, God!" I said, cringing.

"She came to church with her husband and her kid every Sunday," the pastor said, lowering his head.

"That must've been excruciating for you," I said, feeling sorry for him.

"I somehow got through it. It wasn't easy though," the pastor said with a somber expression.

"Did it never bother you that she had premarital sex?" Luca asked inquisitively.

"It's not for me to judge. *'There is only one Lawgiver and Judge, the One who is able to save and to destroy; but who are you who judge your neighbor? James 4:12.'*"

"Still..." I had a hard time believing he wasn't bothered by it all.

"I was terribly upset that she had premarital sex, but I don't hold that against her, and neither does the Lord. She did confess her sin to me during one of our confession sessions."

"Have you considered leaving priesthood?" Luca fired the question out of the blue.

"Yes. If I fall in love with a woman, and I wish to marry her, I will leave the priesthood," the pastor said, fiddling with his rosary.

"I hope you find Miss. Right someday. You deserve it," I said, smiling at him.

"Why thanks!" The pastor said as his eyes lit up.

Luca and I prayed for a few minutes and decided to leave the chapel. We figured the pastor could use some alone time.

"We'll take our leave now," Luca said, putting his hands behind my back.

"See you later, kids," the pastor said in a cheery tone.

"See you later, pastor James," I said, waving at him.

Luca and I walked out of the chapel and exhaled loudly.

"He's human, after all. Not a monster," Luca said with a surprised look on his face.

"Now that's a man with a story. A story of love and heartbreak," I said, awestruck.

"His girlfriend dumped him because he flunked out of medical school. That's harsh," Luca said, clicking his tongue.

"She's the reason he went from becoming a lovesick teenager to an underwear thief," I said, sounding upset.

"What an odd transformation!" Luca said, resting his hands under his chin.

"He seems to have lost all faith in love," I said, looking disappointed.

"That's not true," Luca said, wagging a finger in front of my face.

"Why not?"

"He has faith in God, and God is love," Luca said with a glint in his eyes.

"That's true."

"He'll be alright, right?" Luca asked, sounding doubtful.

"Yeah, he'll be okay," I said, patting him on the back.

"We need to get going now. Don't wanna miss lunch," Luca said, rubbing his tummy.

Luca and I reached the children's home in time for lunch. We had roasted chicken with gooseberry sauce.

"I could have another plate of this. It's so delicious!" I said, licking my plate clean.

"Yeah, we get served this only once a month," Rudolfo said, sighing.

"What a bummer!" Luca said, sulking.

After we had our lunch, we staggered towards my room.

"I don't think I can walk to my room," I said, pressing my hand against my belly.

"Is this another attempt to get me to carry you in my arms? Well, I'm not gonna carry you again, Laura," Luca said, scrunching his nose.

"Very droll, Luca," I said, shaking my head.

"I feel like I'm pregnant," Luca said, groaning.

"That's not possible. You're a boy," I said, guffawing.

"Not an actual baby, idiot. I mean, I'm pregnant with a food baby," Luca said, knocking me on the head.

We somehow made it to my room. As soon as we reached the room, we dived into bed.

"Is it okay if I take a siesta here?" Luca said, making himself comfortable in my bed.

"It's okay. You can sleep here," I said with a warm smile.

Luca soon fell asleep. I lay next to him, gazing into his honey-brown eyes.

"I love you," I whispered in his ear.

"Did you say something?" Luca said with a sudden jerk of his head.

"N-n-no," I said, startled.

I tried staying awake, but I couldn't. I felt dizzy and dozed off a few minutes after Luca fell asleep. When I woke up, it was a quarter past eight at night.

"Oh, Lord! How long have I been sleeping? Luca, wake up," I said, tapping his shoulder.

"Noooo," Luca whined.

"Luca!" I said, jolting him awake.

"Why can't you just let me sleep in peace?" Luca said, sitting up in anger.

"It's a quarter past eight. It's way past dinner time," I said, pouting.

"Oh no! I'm starving though," Luca cried. I could hear his tummy rumbling.

I snuck into the kitchen and saw a basket of stale bruschettas on the kitchen counter. I grabbed it and tiptoed into my room.

"Here! Fill up on this," I said, tossing the basket at him.

"Bruschetta, my favourite!" Luca said, licking his lips and hastily grabbing a few bruschettas in his hands.

"Give me one," I said, snatching the last stale bruschetta from the basket.

"You're the best!" Luca said, kissing me on the cheek.

"Oh-" I covered my blushed face with my hands.

"I'll go to my room now. Sleep tight," Luca said, taking the empty basket with him and heading out of the room.

"Good night, Luca! Sweet dreams," I said, waving him goodbye.

I hopped into bed with a smile of satisfaction. It felt so good to snuggle up to Luca earlier in the day. He smelled of lavender oil. I wanted to sniff his neck and nibble on his ears the entire time he was lying next to me. I knew right then and there that he was the guy I wanted to spend the rest of my life with.

CHAPTER EIGHT

PLEASURE BEGETS PAIN

"For the one who does wrong will be repaid for his wrong, and there are no exceptions." (Colossians 3:25)

When I went to Luca's room the next day, he was whimpering in bed.

"Hey, Luca. What happened? What's wrong?" I asked with a worried look on my face.

"Laura, I hate myself!" Luca said, tears stinging his eyes.

"Please don't say that..." I said, reaching out my hand to wipe his tears.

"You were right. I'm cheating on Giulia," Luca said, hanging his hand in shame.

"With whom?" I asked, sitting beside him in bed.

"You, I can't stop thinking about you," Luca said, looking me straight in the eye.

"I don't know what to say to that," I said, looking away from him.

"Remember I told you yesterday I dreamt about Giulia and my wedding day. I lied," Luca said, biting his bottom lip.

"Well then, who were you dreaming about?" I asked, moving closer to him.

"You. I dreamt of you," Luca said, taking my hands in his.

"What kind of a dream was it?" I asked, wondering what exactly he dreamt of me.

"A wet one. A wet dream," Luca said, his face turning red as a tomato.

"A wet dream?" I asked, looking clueless.

"Yeah, that's why I was in such good spirits yesterday," Luca said, sighing.

"Does a wet dream have something to do with swimming in a stream or a creek?" I asked, tapping my forefinger on my chin.

"Oh, God, no! Stop taking things so literally," Luca said, slapping his forehead.

"Did you pee when you dreamt about me? Is that what a wet dream is?" I asked, chuckling.

"Oh dear, you're as innocent as a lamb. God bless your soul," Luca said, stroking my hair.

"I don't wanna be innocent! What is it then?" I asked, huffing.

"It's a sex dream. I ejaculated while I was sleeping," Luca said, covering his face with his hands.

"Eww! Can a woman have a wet dream?" I asked, my eyes widened.

"Yes," Luca said with a half-smile.

"You dreamt we had sex, didn't you?" I said, shaking a finger at him."Not really. I dreamt of you lying topless in bed in the parsonage," Luca said with a bashful smile.

"After you got blue balls? Gosh, I've done a number on you, haven't I?" I said, resting my hands under my chin.

"You sure have," Luca said with a big goofy grin on his face.

"Do you use lavender oil?" I asked, narrowing my eyes.

"Yes.... Why?" Luca asked, raising his eyebrows.

"When you were lying here yesterday, you smelled of lavender oil," I said, smiling at him.

"Oh, really? I guess I applied too much oil to my body," Luca said, shifting his weight from one foot to the other.

"Can I have some of that lavender oil? It smells so good!" I said, inhaling the sweet scent that still lingered in my room.

"Sure. You can ask me for the oil anytime you want it," Luca said, looking distracted.

"Thanks!" I said with a twinkle in my eye.

"Can we go to the garden now?" Luca asked, really hoping I'd say yes for once.

"Yes!"

We finished our breakfast quickly and dashed to the garden. We played lock and key, and halfway through the game, Luca fell on the ground and soiled his white t-shirt.

"Oh, God!" I rushed to his side. "Are you okay?"

"Yes, I'm okay. I'll tell you who won't be okay - the matron," Luca said, trying to get rid of the stains on his t-shirt.

"Forget about the matron. Here, let me help you," I said, reaching my hand out to him.

I helped him get up to his feet and walked him to my room.

"I'll wash your shirt. Give it to me," I said, opening my bathroom door.

"Okay," Luca said nonchalantly.

Luca removed his t-shirt and time stood still for a second.

"Laura, are you there?" Luca asked, waving the t-shirt in front of my face.

"Uh-huh..."

"Laura, here's the shirt," Luca said, putting the t-shirt in my hands.

"Ah, yeah, right. I was spacing out. Sorry," I said, shaking my head.

I wanted Luca to push me up against the wall and drown me in kisses.

"Are you okay? You seem a little off," Luca said, sounding worried."Yeah, I don't know. I'm just troubled by everything that's been happening here, you know?" I said, rubbing my temple nervously.

"Tell me about it," Luca said, scoffing.

I washed his t-shirt with a bar of old soap and water. It took me nearly twenty minutes to get rid of the stains on his t-shirt.

"Here, it's good as new. You just need to let it dry for a while," I said, handing Luca the t-shirt.

"Thanks, Laura. You're the best! What would I do without you?" Luca said, holding the t-shirt close to his chest.

"You'd be royally screwed without me. You'd probably get whacked to death by the matron," I said, shaking my head.

"Haha. Always with the quips this one," Luca said, jabbing me in the ribs.

"Just helping a friend in need is all," I said with a shrug.

"As a token of gratitude, I'll give you a bottle of that lavender oil you like," Luca said with a smug smile.

"Really?" I said, jumping for joy.

"Yeah. Are you sure you want lavender oil? I have rosemary oil too," Luca said, scratching the back of his neck.

"I'll take the lavender one," I said, putting my hands behind my back.

Luca left the room with his t-shirt and returned a minute later with a bottle of lavender oil.

"Here you go," Luca said, tossing the bottle of lavender oil at me.

"Thanks!" I said, catching the bottle in the air.

"Just ask me if you need more. I have like ten bottles of these," Luca said, stretching his arms.

"See you at lunch, Luca," I said, glancing at the label of the bottle.

"See you then," Luca said, sauntering out of my room.

My heart was hammering in my chest. I bit my bottom lip really hard as I thought of his shirtless body. I took the bottle of lavender oil to sprinkle a few drops of oil on the palm of my right hand. I accidentally emptied the whole bottle in my palm. I was extremely distracted.

"Oh, shit!"

I didn't wanna wash the oil off my hands. The oil looked like it cost a fortune. I applied it to my face, my arms, and my legs, and there was still some excess oil in my hands.

"What's going on with me?"

Suddenly, a dirty thought penetrated my mind. I locked the bedroom door and drew the curtains.

"It should at least be half an hour before I have my lunch."

I got in bed and lay there as still as a mouse. I had never done this before, so I was very nervous.

"There's no backing out now." I shook my head and took a deep breath.

I pulled the blanket up to my neck and pulled my panties down to my ankles.

"Lord, please forgive me for what I'm about to do."

My right hand reached down to my nether region and I started touching myself.

At first, I didn't feel anything, but when images of Luca carrying me in his arms and removing his shirt ran across my mind, I started feeling aroused. Soon, I was moaning loudly.

"This feels so good!" I closed my eyes in pure bliss.

The pleasure was slowly building up, and suddenly it felt like a thousand stars exploded in between my legs. Then, I felt like I was floating on a fluffy white cloud in the clear blue skies.

"Why haven't I done this before?" I wondered, lying spread-eagled.

I quickly got cleaned up and headed to the dining room.

"Somebody woke up on the right side of the bed," Rudolfo said, biting the tines of his fork.

I sat opposite to Luca. I couldn't look him in the eye. I was shy, like a newlywed bride on her wedding night.

"Laura, that lavender has done wonders to your face...You're glowing," Luca said, gaping at me.

"Really? Thanks," I said, touching my face.

"God, your skin is so smooth, and your hands are so soft. Plus, you smell so good. What's the secret?" Rudolfo said, sniffing my hands.

"The lavender oil Luca gave to me," I said, coyly.

"That explains why Luca smells good all the time. It's the lavender oil at work right there," Rudolfo said, waving the fork in Luca's face.

"What are we having for lunch?" I asked, pulling my chair forward.

"Corn and mushroom spaghetti and Chicken parmigiana," Rudolfo said, smacking his lips.

"Can't wait to dig in!" I said, rubbing my hands together.

After lunch, Luca and I went to his room. He closed the door gently and faced me.

"Are you alright, Laura?" Luca asked, lifting my chin.

"Yeah, why are you asking?" I asked, blinking my eyes.

"Your cheeks were beet-red the entire time you were having lunch," Luca said, caressing my cheeks.

"Oh, really?"

"Is something going on? You weren't yourself back there," Luca said, gazing into my eyes.

"I did something, Luca," I said, twiddling my thumbs.

"What?"

"I-I-I-I touched myself," I said, averting my gaze.

"Really? When?"

"Just now before I had lunch," I said, blushing.

"That explains it. How was your first experience?" Luca asked, beaming at me.

"It was amazing, Luca. I felt like I ascended into the heavens and came back to earth," I said, swaying from side to side.

"It's so good. Once you start, you can't stop," Luca said, flashing me a naughty grin.

"Should I confess to the pastor I touched myself this coming Sunday?" I asked with a pouty face.

"No! The pastor will shame you for touching yourself even though he does it all the time," Luca said, shaking me by the shoulder violently.

"Oh, okay. I won't confess to him then," I said, feeling a bit disoriented.

"Atta girl," Luca said, ruffling my hair. "Okay then, I'll go to my room and read a book."

"See you later, nerd," I said, smirking.

I got in bed soon after Luca left the room. I wanted to get some sleep before heading to the chapel later that day. Just as I was drifting to sleep, I saw Giulia standing by my bedroom door, looking lifeless. She seemed as dead as a doornail.

"Giulia...What are you doing here?" I asked, rubbing my eyes.

She slowly approached my bed, her feet floating in the air, slightly above the bedroom floor. Her eyes bore into mine like two red-hot coals.

"What's wrong, Giulia?" I asked, sitting up in bed.

She wrapped her pale hands around my throat and laughed maniacally.

"Please stop, Giulia. You're hurting me!" I cried, flailing my arms.

She tightened her grip around my throat as I continued to plead with her.

"I can't breathe. I can't..." I croaked, the colour draining from my face.

I couldn't understand why she was hurting me for no reason. Then the realization dawned on me at last.

"It was wrong of me to think of your boyfriend and touch myself. I'm sorry, Giulia," I said, gasping for air.

She finally loosened her grip around my throat and backed away from me. She stared daggers at me as she walked out of the room.

"Oh, God. I'm going crazy. I've completely lost it," I mumbled, cradling myself back and forth in bed.

CHAPTER NINE

LADY TREMAINE

"But whoso shall offend one of these little ones which believe in me, it were better for him that a millstone were hanged about his neck, and that he were drowned in the depth of the sea." *(Matthew 18:6)*

Every Friday night at St. Agnes is movie night. The matron plays family-friendly films in the common hall. After having our dinner, we gathered in the common hall at eight on the dot. The film she'd picked for the night was *Cinderella*. Luca and I kept chatting the entire time instead of watching the film. When the scene with the stepmother came on screen, Luca tapped me on the shoulder and pointed at the screen.

"She looks an awful lot like the matron, doesn't she?" Luca whispered in my ear.

"She does. What's the name of the stepmother?" I whispered back.

"Lady Tremaine."

"Golly, she's also cold and cruel, just like our matron," I said with a chuckle.

The matron scowled at us, folding her arms across her chest.

"What is so funny about this film, Laura?"

"Nothing," I said with a poker face.

"Does this young woman's suffering seem funny to you?" The matron asked sternly, pointing at Cinderella on the screen.

"No..."

"Then, why were you giggling with Luca? What were you two talking about?" The matron asked, shifting her gaze from me to Luca.

"We were just saying how you look an awful lot like Lady Tremaine," Luca said, smirking.

"Who is that?" The matron asked with a puzzled expression.

"The stepmother of Cinderella," I said, pointing at the stepmother on the screen.

"So, I look like Cinderella's evil stepmother, is it?" The matron asked, scoffing.

All the other children looked at the screen and then at the matron. They all gasped softly and started giggling.

"She does look like the stepmother," Gianna whispered in another girl's ear.

"I don't want you, troublemakers, causing a ruckus here. Please leave the hall," the matron said, motioning us to stay outside the hall.

Luca and I shuffled outside the hall and waited there till the film was over. After all the children left the common hall, the matron beckoned us to come inside.

"You two distracted everyone here. Do you know that?" The matron said, glaring at us.

"We're sorry, Miss Maria," I said with my fingers crossed behind my back.

"Nobody paid attention to the film. They just whiled away their time commenting on how I looked and behaved like Cinderella's stepmother," the matron said, looking disappointed.

"We won't do it again, Miss Maria," Luca said, crossing his fingers behind his back too.

"Whatever. Switch off all the lights and fans before you leave the room," the matron said, rolling her eyes.

Soon after the matron left the common hall, Luca jumped up and down.

"The matron's arm, did you see that?" Luca asked, hopping around the room like a kangaroo.

"No."

"She had bite marks on her right arm!" Luca said, pointing at his right arm.

"So?"

"You know what that means, right?" Luca said, shaking me by the shoulder.

"No, I don't what that means," I said, stomping my feet in frustration.

"Between you and Giulia, which one of you tends to bite someone's arm when you get angry?" Luca asked, looking in my direction.

"Giulia, she's been doing it ever since she was born. I have more bite marks and scratches on my arms than I can count," I said with outstretched arms.

"The matron had a tiff with Giulia," Luca said, looking unfocused.

"It could have been anyone else too, couldn't it?" I asked dubiously.

"No. I don't know anyone else here who bites people's arms when they get angry," Luca said with a shrug.

"Yeah, right."

"The matron had something to do with her disappearance, Laura," Luca said, throwing his hands up in the air.

"Why do you say that?" I asked, looking lost.

"Look at her. Guilt is written all over her face," Luca said, pointing his thumbs at his face.

"That doesn't prove anything," I said, sulking.

"What about the bite marks? That proves something, doesn't it?" Luca asked, losing his patience.

"I don't know, Luca. It just seems like we're grasping at straws at this point," I said, sighing.

"Look me in the eye and tell me the matron is not guilty," Luca said, facing me with his hands behind his back.

"She's definitely not innocent. That's for sure. But as for her being involved in Giulia's disappearance, it seems like a bit of a reach," I said, scratching my nose.

"Why don't we just go and ask the matron how she got those bite marks on her arm?" Luca asked, motioning me to go to the matron with him.

"Are you nuts, Luca?" I said, glaring at him.

"It doesn't hurt to try," Luca said, shrugging.

"It does hurt. Do you want me to get whipped with a belt again?" I cried.

"You don't ask then. I'll ask," Luca said, annoyed.

"No one's asking anyone anything. Understood?" I asked, taking his hands in mine.

"Yeah...."

"That being said, the matron was acting really suspicious the night of Giulia's disappearance," I said, clicking my tongue.

"Really?"

"I was sleeping in my bed when I heard something heavy being dragged along the floor. I went outside the room and saw the matron dragging a huge sack along the floorboards in the corridor."

"What was inside the sack?" Luca asked inquisitively.

"When I asked her what it was, she said it was a sack of grains. I didn't think anything of it at the time as we did have a huge feast the next day for lunch," I said, brooding.

"Yeah, I remember. We had Arancini, beef stroganoff, rib-eye steak and rice pudding for lunch," Luca said, stoking his chin.

"What if it was not actually a sack of grains?" I asked, lowering my voice.

"I'm sure it was. We did have three dishes that had grains in them like Arancini, beef stroganoff and rice pudding," Luca said, counting on the fingers of his hand.

"What if she purposely asked the cook to prepare those dishes to throw us off the track?" I asked, snapping my fingers.

"I don't think she thought that far ahead," Luca said, seeming unconvinced.

"Why would she drag a sack of grains from the corridor to the kitchen? Wouldn't the sack of grains be directly delivered to the kitchen?" I asked, chewing my nails.

"Yeah, that does seem strange...." Luca said, frowning.

"Why else would she lie about the gardener having an affair with Giulia? She clearly wanted to pin the blame on someone for Giulia's disappearance, and the gardener was her scapegoat."

"She has done something horrendous to Giulia," Luca said, his breath shuddering.

"I wouldn't put it past her," I said with a severe face.

"But then, how do we explain the blood stains on Giulia's white frock," Luca said, scratching his head.

"You said someone raped her. What if it was the matron?" I asked, deep in thought.

"Oh no, no! It was definitely a man," Luca said with conviction.

"Why? Women don't rape, do they?" I asked, raising my eyebrows.

"They do, but it's unlikely," Luca said, shuddering.

"Oh, okay," I said with a blank look on my face.

"We need to get to the bottom of this," Luca said, smashing his fist into his palm.

"Let's leave the room. It's getting late," I said, ushering him outside.

We headed to our rooms, but we stopped in our tracks when we heard the matron whispering to someone on the phone in her office.

"No, no. Nobody here has caught wind of it," the matron said, sounding wary.

"Yes, I'll make sure it stays that way," the matron muttered under her breath.

"I've told the children that Giulia ran away with the gardener. They all fell for it hook, line and sinker," the matron said, roaring with laughter.

"No, it's not stupid. I've asked him to never step foot on the premises ever again," the matron hissed under her breath.

"I just told him I was firing him because he was doing a terrible job at gardening," the matron said with a heavy sigh.

"I'm cleaning up your mess, you know...."

"I didn't pay him a penny, no," the matron said, shaking her head.

"The twin sister doesn't suspect anything. Although she's a pain in the ass," the matron moaned.

"I'll keep an eye on her. Don't worry about it," the matron assured the other speaker.

"Take care. Goodnight," The matron said and ended the call.

We quietly stepped away from the door and tiptoed to my room.

"If that doesn't scream guilty, then I don't know what will," Luca said, grasping the ends of his hair.

"She just confirmed our suspicion that Giulia didn't run away with the gardener," I said, gritting my teeth.

"Who was she talking to on the phone?" Luca asked, pacing about the room anxiously.

"I don't know, but that person is just as if not more guilty than her," I said, grimacing.

"No doubt about that," Luca said with a grim expression.

"While she keeps an eye on me, we should keep an eye on her," I said in a somber tone.

"Definitely," Luca said with a slight nod of the head.

"We've got ourselves a real-life Lady Tremaine," I said, cracking my knuckles.

"At least Lady Tremaine wasn't involved in a child's disappearance," Luca said, fuming.

"She's worse than the stepmother!" I said, balling my fists.

"She sure is," Luca said, sneering. "Get some sleep, Laura. I'll see you tomorrow morning."

"Goodnight, Luca," I said, waving at him.

I got in bed and mulled over the conversation between the matron and the unknown speaker. Who was this stranger? Was it Pastor James, or was it someone else?

CHAPTER TEN

TWO BROKEN HEARTS MAKE A WHOLE

"He heals the brokenhearted and binds up their wounds."
(Psalm 147:3)

When Giulia and I were three years old, our mother gifted us two necklaces. She told us to wear it around our necks at all times, till the day we died. The pendants on our necklaces were of a heart broken in two. I had one half of the broken heart, and Giulia had the other half of the broken heart. Our mother told us that even though we were two individuals in two separate bodies, our hearts beat as one. We felt the same feelings. She said if I rejoiced, she would rejoice too, and if she felt pain, I would feel it too. I have never once removed the necklace from my neck, and neither has Giulia. Whenever I see Giulia's ghost, I see her spirit wearing the necklace.

We're tied to each other forever, both by our blood and by the necklaces. We're one person in two different bodies. When Giulia disappeared, I lost a part of myself. There is a void in my heart that only she can fill. I feel like I'm slowly fading away into nothingness. There are so many things I've done recently that I'm not proud of. I've not done right by Giulia, and I feel terrible about it. I've fallen for Luca, and I know I shouldn't. I'm in love with him, and I hate myself for it. I've betrayed my one and only dear sister. I'm no better than Judas Iscariot.

This morning, I confronted the matron and told her she was a huge liar, and that she would burn in hell for it.

"Giulia didn't run away with the gardener, did she?" I asked, clenching my teeth.

"Why are you bringing this up now, Laura?" The matron asked with a vexed voice.

"Just answer my question. Did Giulia elope with the gardener? Yes or No?" I asked, folding my arms across my chest.

"Yes, she eloped with him. Haven't I already told you that a million times?" The matron said impatiently.

"You're involved in her disappearance, aren't you?" I asked, looking her dead in the eye.

"How on earth did you even come to that conclusion?" The matron asked, raising her hands above her head.

"For all I know, you probably killed my sister!" I said, pointing an accusing finger at her.

"Stop with this nonsense!" The matron barked at me.

The matron snatched the necklace from my neck.

"Give it back to me," I said, standing on tippy toes to reach for the necklace.

"You can get it back when you've learned some manners," the matron said, raising it higher in the air.

"You don't understand. That's the only thing I have to remember my sister by. You can't take it away from me," I said, my eyes swelling with tears.

"You should've thought of that before you ran that filthy mouth of yours," the matron said, sneering.

Luca stepped in front of the matron.

"Give Laura her necklace back," Luca said, raising his voice.

"Don't poke your nose where it doesn't belong," the matron said, glowering.

"This necklace was gifted to her by her mother. Her sister has one too. Her mother told them they must never remove their necklaces. You'd be offending her late mother and her sister by taking that necklace away from her," Luca said with a grim expression.

"Whatever. Get out of my sight," the matron said, tossing the necklace at Luca.

"Thanks, Luca. For a moment there, I was considering murdering her to get my necklace back from her," I said, fuming.

"Well, there's no need to resort to murder now, is there?" Luca said, smiling at me.

After breakfast, Luca and I were taking a stroll in the garden when Rudolfo came running towards us, panting.

"Guys, Mr. Lorenzo has come. He wants to meet all of us," Rudolfo said, wheezing.

Mr. Lorenzo was the owner of the children's home. He was a prominent philanthropist in his late forties. It was thanks to him we had a roof over our heads, comfortable beds to lie in, and three-square meals every day. Mr. Lorenzo was the antithesis of Miss Maria. He was the sweetest man on planet earth. He wouldn't even hurt a fly.

We all assembled in the common hall. Luca and I elbowed our way to the front of the room.

"Did you have your breakfast?" Lorenzo asked, placing six-year-old Emiliano, one of the kids in our children's home, on his lap.

"Yes," Emiliano said, beaming at him.

"What did you have?" Lorenzo asked, booping his nose.

"We had Frittatas and Cappuccinos," Emiliano said, squirming on his lap.

"Did you like them?" Lorenzo asked, lifting his chin.

"Yes. I love all the meals served here!" Emiliano replied with a sparkle in his eye.

"I make sure you kids get nothing but the best. If it were up to the matron, she'd serve you all nothing but stale gruel and apples three times a day," Mr. Lorenzo said, grinning at the matron.

"The children already hate me, sir. No need to make them hate me more," the matron said, scowling at him.

"Nobody hates her more than me," I said, tittering.

"Cheeky brat!" the matron muttered under her breath.

"What is your name, dear?" Mr. Lorenzo asked, motioning me to step forward.

"Laura," I said, putting my arms behind my back.

"Laura, huh? That's a beautiful name," Mr. Lorenzo said, gazing into my eyes.

"Thanks!" I responded with a warm smile.

"Are you the girl whose twin sister went missing six months ago?" Mr. Lorenzo asked, raising his eyebrows.

"Yes...."

"The matron told me all about it. She ran away with the gardener, didn't she?" Mr. Lorenzo said with a heavy sigh.

"No."

"Then what happened to her?" Mr. Lorenzo asked with a concerned look on his face.

"I believe she was murdered," I said in a somber tone.

"Murdered? By whom?" Mr. Lorenzo asked, looking alarmed.

"I don't know who it is yet, but I know she was killed for sure," I said, averting my gaze.

"One twin can sense when the other twin is in danger. You might not be wrong, but you must keep your hopes up, dear. Her dead body wasn't found, was it?"

"No."

"Then she could be alive. Let's not jump to conclusions, yeah?" Mr. Lorenzo said, tousling my hair.

I wanted to tell Mr. Lorenzo about Giulia's ghost, but I was afraid he'd think I was crazy, so I kept my mouth shut.

"It was nice meeting you, kids. I have to go now. There's an important meeting I must attend in the next town. I'll see you all soon. Stay safe and stay healthy."

We all huddled by the entrance gate as he drove his sleek black Fiat out of the estate.

"He is a great man, but God bless his poor lungs," Luca said, joining his hands together.

"He reeked of cigarette smoke. I could smell the smoke in his breath," I said, wrinkling my nose.

"The man's a chain smoker," Luca said, coughing.

"We all have bad habits. His is smoking," I said, shrugging.

"The matron even has the owner fooled about Giulia's disappearance," Luca said in disbelief.

"I know. He doesn't believe she was murdered," I said, sulking.

"He's trying to be optimistic. Can't blame him," Luca said, smiling wistfully.

"Yeah...I don't know if I'm crazy for even thinking this, but what if it was the owner who murdered Giulia," I said in a very low voice.

"No, that's not possible. He just told us he believes she is still alive," Luca said, his eyes widened.

"That's what a murderer would say. Try to convince us she's alive when he knows full well she's dead," I said, balling my fists.

"Mr. Lorenzo visits the children's home only once a month, and that too in the mornings. Giulia disappeared at night, didn't she? She was there with us that morning," Luca said, lost in thought.

"Yeah."

"The matron, on the other hand, is always here at St. Agnes. I'm sure she's the culprit," Luca said, shaking his finger at me.

"But she was talking to someone else on the phone last night, remember? That person is certainly involved in Giulia's disappearance too. Who do you think that was?" I asked, moving closer to him.

"My guess is it was the pastor," Luca said, stroking his chin.

"I thought that too," I said, snapping my fingers.

"The matron and the pastor don't exactly get along, but the matron and the owner are like cat and dog," Luca said, facing me.

"It makes sense her partner in crime is someone she can mildly put up with," I said, brooding.

"Exactly."

"The matron probably knows the pastor is a pedophile. She helped him cover up the crime," I said, shaking my head.

"According to her, it doesn't matter how bad a person is as long as that person is a man of the cloth," Luca said, rolling his eyes.

"I wouldn't be surprised if the matron is sleeping with the pastor," I said, grimacing.

"What? Why would you say that?" Luca asked, looking surprised.

"It's obvious. The way she flirts with him whenever she talks to him," I said, looking disgusted.

"She does, doesn't she?"

"And he probably gave her the bite marks on her arm," I said, pointing to my right arm.

"Didn't we say Giulia gave them to the matron?" Luca asked, looking muddled.

"We don't know that sure," I said with a shrug.

"I'm not sure I buy this theory," Luca said, scratching his head.

"The matron has been deprived of a man's touch all her life, and pastor James is a very fine-looking man," I said, whistling.

"He is. He looks like a movie star, doesn't he?" Luca said, dreamy-eyed.

"His third option should have been to become an actor. When medicine and priesthood fail, he could always try his hand at acting."

"How old is the pastor?" Luca asked, placing a hand on my shoulder.

"I'm not sure of the exact number, but I think he's in his late twenties," I said with uncertainty.

"And the matron is in her early thirties," Luca said with a straight face.

"Yeah."

"For all that talk of chastity, I don't think the matron is a chaste woman herself," Luca said, scorning.

"Neither is the pastor," I said, incensed.

"What a bunch of hypocrites! Telling us to save ourselves for marriage when they're doing the exact opposite of that," Luca said with utmost contempt.

"I know, right?"

"Let's go inside, shall we?" Luca said, pulling me closer to him and enveloping me in a warm embrace.

"Yes, it's freezing out here," I said, shaking like a leaf.

We went to my room and took a short nap. We spooned each other and wished we could stay like that forever.

Part Two (Luca Bianchi)

Seven Years Later.....

CHAPTER ELEVEN

ON OUR OWN

'On hearing this, Jesus said to them, "It is not the healthy who need a doctor, but the sick. I have not come to call the righteous, but sinners."' (Mark 2:17)

When Laura and I turned 18, we had to leave St. Agnes. We packed our bags and set out from Maranello to Modena. We were glad we were never gonna see the matron and the creepy pastor ever again. But our life outside the children's home was even worse than our life inside it. Neither of us was qualified for a decent job. We never went to college or school, and the education we received in the children's home was a theological-based one, so that was of no good use in the real world.

The only jobs we were qualified for were minimum-wage jobs. I got a job as a bag boy at a grocery store, and Laura got a job as a waitress at a local diner. We both worked two shifts. My first shift started at 7 in the morning and ended at noon, and my second shift started at four in the evening and ended at eight at night. Laura's first shift began at nine in the morning and ended at noon, and her second shift began at nine in the night and ended at midnight. I didn't like that Laura had to stay out so late at night.

We lived in a dangerous neighbourhood. There were a lot of druggies, drunkards, ex-convicts, and homeless people roaming the streets at night. Since we couldn't afford to pay the rent for a proper apartment, we had to rent a cheap apartment. The rent for the apartment cost seventy euros per month and that was all we could afford to pay for the time being. Even though we pulled double shifts and saved what little we could, it seemed as though were more broke than when we started working. Sometimes, we would skip lunch and dinner and eat only our breakfast to save money. It was not healthy, but we had no other choice. We had only two options: either we eat all three meals a day and burn a hole in our pockets, or we skip two meals a day from time to time and have enough money to pay our rent on time. We obviously chose the latter.

I liked working as a bag boy at the grocery store. It was not ideal, but it was satisfactory. I would come across different types of people from different walks of life every day. Just the other day, I helped an old lady with her groceries. I carried them all the way to her car. She told me that God would bless me for the good deed that I'd done for her. It's so fulfilling to help those in need.

One of my co-workers, Adriana, is six months pregnant. She wobbles her way around the store. I asked her one day where the father of the baby was. She told me that her baby daddy left her after she told him she was pregnant with his child. It must be really difficult raising a child all by yourself. I can't imagine abandoning Laura if she was pregnant with my child. A man who doesn't take care of the mother of his child is not a man. He is a monster! Whenever Adriana skips her breakfast, I buy her a granola bar or a bar of chocolate from the grocery store with the money I saved from skipping my breakfast. With a baby on the way, she simply can't afford to skip her meals.

Adriana is only seventeen, a year younger than me. Her parents kicked her out of their house when she told them she was pregnant with her ex-boyfriend's baby. She now lives in a rundown apartment all by herself. All the money she earns at the grocery store goes towards paying her monthly rent, so she has no other go but to skip her meals now and then. Since she has no brother and is an only child, I'm like the elder brother she never had. I'm also very protective of her.

One day, a lady came to the checkout and saw Adriana stroking her belly. She asked her how old she was. Adriana told her she was seventeen, and the woman was stunned. She asked if Adriana was married, and Adriana shook her head.

"Shame on you for having a child out of wedlock. You're gonna burn in hell, missy," the woman said, shaking a finger at her.

When Adriana heard this, she started bawling like a child. I rushed to her side and asked her what was wrong. When Adriana told me what the woman said, I gave the woman a piece of my mind.

"Not everyone's life is smooth and sailing like yours. Judging by the expensive fur coat you're wearing, you don't exactly seem to know what it's like to live on minimum wage. If your daughter had a child out of wedlock, you can afford to get rid of it or spoil the child and give it everything it needs. This woman here doesn't have that luxury, you see, ma'am."

"Don't take this wretched woman's side, young man," the woman said, glaring at her.

"Why are you so quick to blame the woman? Why not blame the father of the child?" I asked, annoyed.

"He's not the one who's pregnant, is he?" The woman said, sizing her up.

"You're a woman. You should know better than to shame another woman," I said, shaking my head.

"You'll go to hell if you take this sinner's side. I'm warning you," the woman said, scorning.

"If standing up for this young girl is the reason I go to hell, then so be it. Besides, didn't Jesus take the side of the sinners and not of the self-righteous people?"

"So, you think you're Jesus, huh?" The woman asked, sneering.

"No, I didn't say that. As Christians, we're supposed to be following in his footsteps, aren't we?" I asked, looking disappointed.

"I'm a better Christian than this young lady will ever be," the woman said, huffing.

"And how exactly do you know that? It's this holier-than-thou attitude that Christ couldn't stand," I said, clicking my tongue.

"I'm gonna report you to the manager," the woman said menacingly.

"Go ahead, report me. Hope you get a good night's sleep knowing you got a minimum wage worker fired," I said, scowling at her.

"See you never," the woman said, throwing her hands up in the air.

"See you in hell," I said, smirking. Fortunately, the lady didn't hear me. If she did, I would've ended up in a world of trouble.

After the lady stormed out of the store, Adriana flung her arms around me.

"You didn't have to do that, Luca," Adriana said, blubbering.

"She had it coming. I was just doing what any guy would do," I said, smiling at her.

"No guy would've done what you just did. You put your job on the line to defend me," Adriana said, sniveling.

"I wouldn't have it any other way," I said, pinching her cheeks.

Adriana and I were the last ones to leave the store after our morning shift. I bought her an orange soda and was sitting beside her behind the checkout counter when Adriana leaned in for a kiss.

"Why did you do that?" I asked, touching my face in shock and disbelief.

"I'm so sorry, Luca. I just got caught up in the moment," Adriana said, looking away from me out of pure shame.

"I see you like my younger sister. I don't have feelings for you. This can't happen again," I said, moving away from her.

"I know. It's just my pregnancy hormones are making me do things I wouldn't do otherwise," Adriana said, her face turning red.

"It's okay. Just don't do it again," I said with a half-smile.

"Sure."

"I haven't told you this, but I have a girlfriend," I said, rubbing the back of my neck.

"Oh, really?"

"Hm-mmm. We've known each other for a lifetime," I said as my eyes lit up.

"I must say, she's one lucky woman to have a guy like you," Adriana said, smiling wistfully.

"Oh, come on."

"I really mean it. My ex-boyfriend is a major douche. To think I'm carrying his baby," Adriana said, fuming.

"Forget about him. You'll find a nice guy. Trust me," I said, giving her a pat on the back.

"Who'll want me? I'm all used goods. No man wants a woman who has a baby from another man," Adriana said with a pouty face.

"You'll be surprised. Some men are willing to look past such things. Not all men are douches," I said, grinning at her.

"Says the only guy I know who is not a douche," Adriana said, playfully nudging my arm. "Anyhoo, I have to get going now. My feet are swollen. I need to take a good hot shower and soak my feet in warm water."

"See you tomorrow. Take care, Adriana," I said as I headed out of the store.

"You too," Adriana said, waving at me.

After I got to the apartment, I slept for a short while. Laura returned home an hour later. The grocery store is only a few blocks away from the apartment, so I go come home on foot. The diner where Laura works is at least two miles away from the apartment, so she has to catch a bus to get home.

"I'm dead tired," Laura said, stretching her arms.

"Me too," I said, stifling a yawn.

"I'm gonna hop in the shower," Laura said with a tired smile.

"Before you go, there's something I need to tell you," I said in a very low voice.

"What's it?" Laura asked, looking concerned.

"You know Adriana, right?" I asked, twiddling my thumbs.

"The teen mom?" Laura asked, raising her eyebrows.

"Yes. A woman shamed her for being a teen mom and told her she'd go to hell. I stood up for her. After our shift got over, we were chatting about what happened earlier when she kissed me."

"Kissed you on the lips?" Laura asked, narrowing her eyes.

"Yes......"

"Why are you telling me this?" Laura asked, folding her arms across her chest.

"Just thought I should let you know. I turned her down right then and there and told her I have a girlfriend," I said, biting my bottom lip.

"Okay," Laura said with a blank expression.

"Aren't you mad at me?" I asked, scratching my neck.

"No. Why would I be mad at you?" Laura asked, shrugging.

"Because she kissed me, Laura!" I said, raising my voice.

"So? If I were in her place, I would've kissed you too. It's too bad she doesn't have a loving boyfriend like mine," Laura said, looking at me with tender affection.

"Am I hearing this right?" I asked, putting my hands behind my ears.

"I'm so proud of what you did today, Luca. You're the epitome of a gentleman," Laura said, holding my face in her hands.

"Really?"

"You stood up for that pregnant girl when no one else did, and you turned down her advances. Could I have asked for a better boyfriend than you?" Laura said, resting her forehead against mine.

"Any other woman would've ripped my head off if I told her what I just told you," I said, gaping at her.

"I'm not like other women, am I?" Laura asked with a smug smile.

"Definitely not," I said in wide-eyed wonder.

"I'm gonna get in the shower," Laura said, trudging towards the bedroom.

"Can I join you?" I asked, grabbing her arm.

"What? You wanna shower with me?" Laura asked, her eyes widened.

"Yes. There's always a first time for everything," I said with a coy smile.

"No naughty business, okay? We're not having sex till we get married," Laura said, eyeing me suspiciously.

"Clearly," I said, looking at her like a mischievous child.

I followed her to the bathroom. We hopped out of our sweaty clothes and got into the shower.

"This is gonna be the ultimate test in self-control," Laura said with a heavy sigh.

"And Lord knows it's not gonna be easy," I said, rubbing my temple.

CHAPTER TWELVE

THE SAPPHIRE RING

"But if they cannot control themselves, they should marry, for it is better to marry than to burn with passion." (1 Corinthians 7:9)

We were washing our bodies under the showerhead when I grabbed a bar of soap and pushed Laura up against the bathroom wall. I soaped my hands and thrust my hands inside her snatch.

"You like this, huh?" I asked, gazing into her hazel eyes.

"Oh, God!" Laura gasped loudly.

I rubbed her pleasure nub with my fingers till she came. Then, she pulled me closer to her and grabbed my cazzo. She soaped it and stroked it repeatedly till I came on her thighs.

"God, that feels so good!" I said, closing my eyes and breathing heavily.

"I feel dirty," Laura said, rubbing her hands all over her body.

"That's ironic, but I get what you mean," I said, grinning widely.

"It feels like we just had sex," Laura said, her face turning beet-red. I couldn't look him straight in the eye.

"But we didn't though," I said, stroking her hair.

"You think we've sinned?" Laura asked in a very low voice.

"No. As long as we don't have sex, we should be fine," I said, lifting her chin.

We washed each other, got out of the shower, and got dressed for the day.

"We should do it again sometime," Laura said, beaming at me.

"Definitely."

"Why did you wanna shower with me all of a sudden?" Laura asked, narrowing her eyes.

"When Adriana kissed me, I thought of you. Calling you my girlfriend in front of her turned me on for some reason," I said with a bashful smile.

"Well, aren't I one lucky girlfriend? Why don't you get some rest? Your second shift starts at four, right?" Laura asked, glancing at her worn-out brown leather watch.

"Let's watch some TV. I'm bored," I said, groaning.

"You have to sleep, dear," Laura said, holding my face in her hands.

"I don't wanna sleep though. We just got intimate in the shower. It would only be right to cuddle together and watch some TV after," I said, pouting like a kid.

"Okay. But this won't always work, mister," Laura said, shaking a finger at me.

"Noted," I said, smirking.

We snuggled together on the couch and watched *La piovra* on the crap picture box we call TV.

"I'm getting sleepy. I'm going to bed," Laura said, stifling a yawn.

"Me too. I'll join you," I said, following her to the bedroom.

We woke up at half past five and Luca got dressed for work

"I'll see you later tonight," Luca said, buttoning his beige-coloured shirt.

"Yeah."

"Should we do it again tonight?" I said, putting on his blue vest and cap.

"We only do it once a day. Don't push it, mister," Laura said, tugging at his earlobes.

"Oh, noooo! You're killing me, Laura," I said, looking disappointed.

"Okay. See you at night. Take care, dear," Laura said, caressing my cheeks.

"Take care, Laura," I said as I opened the main door.

I went to the grocery store in less than five minutes. Adriana was working the counter.

"Hi, Luca," Adriana said, swaying from side to side.

"Hey, Adriana," I greeted her.

"I have some good news," Adriana said, putting her hands behind her back.

"What is it?" I asked, looking surprised.

"There's a really sweet guy at my church. He wants to be my boyfriend!" Adriana said, jumping for joy.

"Isn't that wonderful? Didn't I tell you you'd find a nice guy?" I asked, unable to contain my excitement.

"Yeah..."

"I have some good news of my own," I said, scratching my ear.

"It just better and better, doesn't it?" What's the good news?" Adriana asked, clapping her hands.

"I'm proposing to my girlfriend tonight," I said, grinning from ear to ear.

"Oh my, have you picked a ring and everything?" Adriana asked, wonderstruck.

"Yes, I saved up some money and bought a sapphire ring for her."

"Does she like sapphire?" Adriana asked inquisitively.

"Yes, she likes all things blue," I said, smiling at her.

"Then she's definitely gonna love it," Adriana said with a gleam in her eye.

"I should've gone for gold. I feel like a cheapskate," I said, heaving a sigh.

"Nonsense! Gold is overrated. Sapphire is perfect. Believe me," Adriana said, placing a hand on my shoulder.

We worked at the counter for the next four hours. We clocked out at sharp eight.

"See you tomorrow morning," Adriana said, waving at me.

"See you then, Adriana," I said, waving back at her,

I got home and changed into my nightdress. I waited impatiently for her to return home. When she got home, I switched off all the lights in the living room.

"Hello, are you there, Luca?" Laura asked, sounding wary.

She carefully treaded through the living room. When she opened the bedroom door, I sprung from behind the door.

"Ahhh!" Laura leaped like a cat.

"Surprise!" I said, doing jazz hands.

"Shit, you scared me, Luca!" Laura said, holding her hands on her chest.

"Welcome back, dear," I said, with outstretched arms.

"Don't ever do that again!" Laura said, hugging me.

"Aren't you gonna ask me why I switched off all the lights in the living room?" I asked with a big grin on my face.

"Why on earth did you do that?" Laura asked, scoffing.

"For this."

I got on my knees and pulled out the case from my breast pocket.

"Make me the luckiest man on earth by saying yes, Laura," I said with a glint of hope in my eyes.

"Uhhh...Luca." Laura was at a loss for words.

"Just say yes, dear," I said, my heart in my throat.

"Yes! A thousand times yes!" Laura said, jumping up and down.

I slipped the sapphire ring into her finger and Laura flung her arms around me.

"Make me the luckiest woman on earth by joining me in the shower," Laura said with a seductive voice.

We got undressed and hopped into the shower.

"You're full of surprises, dear," I whistled.

"I love the Sapphire ring, Luca. I love everything blue," Laura said, looking at the ring on her finger.

"I know. That's why I got you the Sapphire ring," I said, holding her hand in mine.

"You know me so well," Laura said, kissing me softly on the lips.

I kissed her neck and cupped her tette with my hands.

"I love you..." Laura whispered in my ear.

"I love you too, Laura," I said, pushing aside a strand of hair from her face.

When I heard Laura those three words, my heart started beating fast. I turned her around and started rubbing myself against her.

"Be careful, dear," Laura said, looking behind her.

Just as I was about to cum, I moved away from her.

"That was a close call," Laura said, panting,

We hopped out of the shower, got dressed, and slipped into bed.

"We should get married soon," I said, putting my hands behind the back of my head.

"I know. I don't think I can take this any longer," Laura said, shaking her head.

"All I want to do right now is have sex with you," I said, biting my bottom lip.

"Me too. We should marry before we sin against the Lord," Laura said, looking worried.

"I agree," I said with a slight nod.

"How about by the end of this month?" Laura asked, moving closer to me.

"That sounds good," I said with a warm smile.

"How was work?" Laura asked, fiddling with her ring.

"It was okay. Adriana has hit the jackpot," I said, fiddling with her necklace.

"Why? What about her?" Laura asked, raising her eyebrows.

"There's a guy at her church who likes her. He wants to be her boyfriend," I said, grinning.

"Aww! She should go for him," Laura said, dreamy-eyed.

"I know. It seems like it's meant to be."

"He may be nice, but he's no Luca though," Laura said, simpering.

"Oh, come here," I said, pulling her close to me.

I tickled her stomach till she was out of breath.

"Stop it, Luca!" Laura said, wheezing.

I unhooked her bra and slipped my hands underneath.

"What are you doing, dear?" Laura asked, her face flushing.

I caressed her warm breasts, squeezed the tips of her pink nips and planted gentle kisses on the back of her neck.

"What did I do to deserve you, dear?" I asked, breathing into her neck.

She put her hands on mine and moaned softly.

"I can't wait to become Mrs. Bianchi. Mrs. Laura Bianchi," Laura said, breathing heavily.

"I can't wait to make you my wife," I said, pressing my feet against hers.

I fell asleep with my hands on her bare bosom. When I woke up an hour later, she was nowhere to be seen. She had gone to work. The bed felt suddenly cold and empty without her in it.

CHAPTER THIRTEEN

RANCID MILK, ROTTEN EGGS, AND OVERRIPE BANANAS

"But if we have food and clothing, we will be content with that."
(1 Timothy 6:8)

When Laura returned home after her night shift, she caught a whiff of the dinner and gagged.

"I wanna throw up," Laura said, pinching her nose.

"Not this again," I said, scowling at her.

"Are you serving a dead raccoon for dinner?" Laura asked, scrunching her nose.

"No!"

"Then why does it smell so bad?" Laura said, retching.

"Stop being so melodramatic," I said, rolling my eyes.

"Every day, it's the same thing. Rancid milk, rotten eggs, and overripe bananas," Laura said, recoiling in disgust.

"Too bad we don't have a plethora of foods like we did in the children's home," I said, staring daggers at her.

"It doesn't have to be grand. It just shouldn't smell like a moffetta's ass," Laura said, wrinkling her nose.

"I eat this moffetta's ass every day for breakfast, lunch, and dinner," I said, sounding upset.

"Well then, good for you," Laura said, throwing her hands up in the air.

"You don't get to eat chicken parmigiana and bruschetta on minimum wage," I said with a chuckle.

"You don't think I know that?" Laura said, frowning.

"Then what do you want?" I asked, boring my eyes into hers.

"Day-old apples instead of these overripe bananas would be good. Some stale buttered bread instead of these rotten eggs and some decent coffee instead of this godawful sour milk!"

"Why don't I serve you some seared beef tenderloin and roasted potatoes on a silver platter instead," I said with a strong dose of sarcasm.

"Don't be sarcastic, Luca," Laura said, scorning.

"Seriously, what do you want me to do?" I asked with a severe expression.

"I don't know. Maybe be more understanding," Laura said with a shrug.

"You think I want to eat this skunk's ass? We have no other choice," I said, moping.

"We always have a choice," Laura said with a half-smile.

"Oh, really?" I asked, looking amused.

"We could always starve," Laura said, gazing into my eyes.

"You'd rather starve to death than eat this?" I asked, raising my eyebrows.

"Yes."

"You're unbelievable, Laura...." I said, shaking my head.

"Oh, come on, Luca. Stop pretending like our life is perfect," Laura said, stomping her feet.

"Our life is not perfect, Laura. But I'm willing to make do with what little we have," I said, looking away from her.

"You shouldn't settle for less, Luca. That's when we give up on life," Laura said with a sullen expression.

"Why did you settle for me then?" I asked, hurting.

"What are you saying?" Laura asked, looking lost.

"Couldn't you have run away with that guy, Rudolfo? His grandparents are filthy rich. He would have pampered you and given you everything you ever dreamt of."

"I didn't run away with Rudolfo because I don't love him. I love you, Luca!" Laura said, tears stinging her eyes.

"Do you though?" I asked, sulking.

"Are you seriously asking me that?" Laura asked, her voice cracking.

"If you settle for me, rancid milk, bad eggs, and overripe bananas are all you're gonna get," I said in a somber tone.

"No, Luca."

"It's not too late to leave me, Laura. You're still very young. Go find yourself a rich guy and marry him," I said, unable to look her in the eye.

"Please don't say that..." Laura said, squeezing my arm.

"I really mean it, dear," I said, tears welling up in my eyes.

"You wouldn't speak this way to Giulia, would you?" Laura asked, wiping her tears with the back of her hand.

"Why are you bringing her up now?" I asked, annoyed.

"You just want to marry me because I look like her. Isn't that the truth?" Laura asked, sniffling.

"Oh, yes. That's exactly what's happening!" I said, glaring at her.

"If Giulia asked for some decent food, wouldn't you give it to her?" Laura asked, looking me dead in the eye.

"Yes. If I have the money, then yes," I said, clenching my teeth.

"It's not about the money, Luca. You can get decent food with minimum wage," Laura said, lowering her voice.

"Then why don't you take charge of buying the food for us from now on?" I asked, folding my arms across my chest.

"I don't mind it," Laura said, smiling to herself.

"Let me see how you manage," I said, sneering.

"I'd do a better job at it than you," Laura said, smugly.

"I'll be the judge of that, dear," I said, lifting her chin.

"You're going to take back every word you said," Laura said, staring at me.

"We'll see about that," I said, heading for the main door. "I have to go now."

"Go on then. You can't wait to see that pregnant whore, can you?" Laura asked, grimacing.

"Who are you calling a pregnant whore?" I asked, completely taken aback by shock.

"You can drop the act. I know you flirt with her," Laura said, baring her teeth.

"I just told you I turned her down yesterday," I said with a blank look on my face.

"You're probably screwing her on that dirty counter where you work," Laura said, giving me a dirty look.

"Shut up, Laura!" I screamed, covering both my ears.

"Did you get her pregnant? Is that why you feel so bad for her?" Laura asked, shoving me.

"What the hell? She was already three months pregnant when I started working there," I said, moving away from her.

"Yeah, yeah, whatever," Laura said, holding up the palm of her hand.

"You said you were fine when I said she kissed me," I said, looking muddled.

"Of course, I'm not fine, Luca. You don't know the first thing about a woman's mind?" Laura asked, pacing about the room furiously.

"Clearly not."

"You got in the shower with me because you were so turned on by Adriana. That's what you said," Laura said, turning to face me.

"No! What the heck? That was not what I said. God, dang it!" I said, banging my fists on the dining table.

"You saw her in me when you came on my thighs," Laura said, grabbing me by the collar of my shirt.

"Laura, one more word out of you, and I'll do something I'll regret," I said, balling my fists.

"Go ahead. You don't like it when I say the truth, huh? Guess what, the truth is always bitter, darling," Laura said, tapping my cheeks.

I slapped her across her face so hard I left a handprint on her right cheek. That was the first and last time I hit Laura.

"How dare you slap your fiancée? So much for being a gentleman," Laura said, touching her cheek.

"You kept pushing my buttons. What did you expect?" I snapped at her.

"Would you have slapped Giulia?" Laura asked, weeping.

"Always going on and on about Giulia," I said, scoffing.

"Giulia is a part of me. You may have forgotten about her, but I can't just forget about her," Laura said, holding her hands on her chest.

"Who says I've forgotten about her? I think about her every single day," I said, brooding.

"Of course, you do," Laura said, huffing.

"You're jealous of your dead sister. You're so pathetic, Laura," I said, clicking my tongue.

"Of course, I'm jealous of her. She dodged a bullet unlike me," Laura said, looking down at the floor.

"I'm a bullet? Are you hearing the words coming out of your mouth?" I asked in disbelief.

"I can't marry you, Luca," Laura said, shaking her head like a toddler.

"You're choosing good food over me. Are you for real right now?" I asked, shaking her by the shoulder.

"It's not about the food. You just slapped me. How can I live with an abuser for the rest of my life?" Laura asked, removing my hand from her shoulder.

"An abuser? Jesus!" I said, my eyes bulging.

"What else should I call you? Prince Charming?" Laura asked, snarling.

"You've lost yourself, Laura. You need help," I said, taking a deep breath.

"I'm the one who needs help?" Laura asked, giving me the death glare.

"Yes."

"Take your awful ring before you leave," Laura said, flinging the ring at me.

"Why did I waste all my money on this ring? It seems like such a waste right now," I said, pouting.

"Who buys a sapphire ring? It's gold or nothing else," Laura said, sounding displeased.

"Yeah, gold ring and expensive food. You should be marrying the Sultan, not me," I said in a mocking tone.

"I don't care about the money, Luca. I care about you," Laura said, taking my hand in hers.

"I care about you too. But I don't have the money to show just how much I care about you," I said, tenderly wiping the tears from her face.

"I don't want fancy food. I want palatable food is all. We can live on bread and water if that's okay with you," Laura said, placing a hand on my chest.

"That's fine by me," I said, putting my arms around her waist.

"I don't wanna lose you, Luca," Laura said, catching a sob in her throat.

"Neither do I, dear," I said, stroking her hair.

"Let's just put this behind us, okay?" Laura asked, smiling at me.

"It's water under the bridge," I said, smiling back at her.

"I'm sorry about what I said earlier about Adriana. That was uncalled for," Laura said, hanging her head in shame.

"You called her a 'pregnant whore,'" I said, gawking at her.

"I know. That was not okay. I know you don't love her like that," Laura said, giving me a peck on the lips.

"No, I don't. I see her as my little sister. Why else do you think I turned her down?" I said, squeezing her shoulder.

"I'm sorry, dear," Laura said, resting her head on my shoulder.

"You're worse than a pregnant woman with crazy hormones," I said, resting my left hand under my chin.

"I may not be a pregnant woman with crazy hormones, but I am a woman on her period," Laura said, grinning at me.

"That explains it," I said, smirking.

"You're a jerk," Laura said, elbowing me.

"See you later, darling," I said, tousling her hair.

"Ciao," Laura said, blowing me a kiss.

As soon as I left, Laura tossed the eggs and the bananas in the trash. She poured her glass of sour milk into the sink. She watched the milk swirl down the drain with a smile of satisfaction.

CHAPTER FOURTEEN

WHO KILLED GIULIA?

"Do not take revenge, my dear friends, but leave room for God's wrath, for it is written: "It is mine to avenge; I will repay," says the Lord." (Romans 12:19)

After we got back home from our night shift, we hit the hay. We were too tired to ask each other how our day went. These double shifts will be the death of us. The next day, I woke up at dawn. It was really dark and quiet in the bedroom. Laura was lying beside me. She looked so peaceful when she slept. I didn't wanna wake her up, so I quietly got out of bed and tiptoed to the living room. I turned on the television and was watching *Lucky Luke* when Laura joined me on the couch.

"You didn't sleep last night?" Laura asked, squeezing my arm.

"I did. I just didn't wanna sleep till five. Thought I'd get an early start," I said with a tired smile.

"The early bird catches the worm as they say," Laura said, smiling at me.

"Right. Why did you wake up now?" I asked, moving closer to her.

"I couldn't sleep properly last night. I had night terrors and broke out in a cold sweat," Laura said, her teeth chattering.

"Night terrors again? Was it about Giulia?" I asked, placing a hand on her inner thigh.

"Uh-huh."

"What was it about?" I asked, concerned.

"She was trying to tell me who killed her, but she couldn't say a word," Laura said, looking troubled.

"That's awful! Giulia's killer hasn't been brought to justice. He or she is still out there roaming the streets and sleeping comfortably in bed without an inch of remorse," I said, gritting my teeth.

"I wish I knew what she was trying to tell me...." Laura said with a heavy sigh.

"We're gonna find out her killer no matter what happens," I said, taking her hands in mine.

"I hope so," Laura said despondently.

"There must be some obvious clue leading to the killer's identity that we aren't noticing," I said, tapping my foot against the floorboard anxiously.

"What would that be?" Laura asked, sounding surprised.

"Describe how you see your twin in your night terrors," I said, gazing into her eyes.

"She walks in the open grasslands wearing her white frock. There's a huge blood stain on the white frock. Near the nether region. Her lips are bleeding and her wrists are bruised."

"Does she have any other wounds on her body?" I asked, sounding distressed.

"Yes, plenty. She has bite marks and scratch marks on her neck and cigarette burns on both of her arms."

"Cigarette burns you say?" I asked, raising my eyebrows.

"Yes. Her killer has pressed the cigarette butt into her flesh causing the nasty burns," Laura said, wincing.

"Interesting......" I said, deep in thought.

The person living in the room opposite ours always smoked. There was that horrid smoke smell wafting in the air in the corridor of the apartment.

"Our neighbour's a chain smoker, isn't he?" I asked, stroking my chin.

"Yeah, I think so. Why?" Laura asked, looking unbothered.

I closed my eyes and inhaled the strong smell of cigarette smoke.

"I know who killed Giulia," I said with a grim visage.

"What? Really?" Laura asked, her hands flying to her chest.

"The clue was right under our noses the entire time. How could we've not noticed that?" I said, frustrated with myself.

"Who is it?" Laura asked in a shaky voice.

"I have to go now. Talk to you later," I said, springing up from the couch.

"Luca, answer me. Who killed Giulia?" Laura asked, raising her voice.

I stormed to the kitchen and grabbed a butcher knife from the counter.

"What in God's name are you doing, Luca?" Laura screamed, grasping the ends of her hair.

"Stay out of this, Laura," I said, shoving her aside.

I left the apartment and headed to the bus stop. Laura chased after me, panting.

"Tell me what's going on," Laura said, catching her breath.

"I can't. No time to talk now," I said, shaking my head.

"Throw me a bone, dear," Laura said, breathing heavily.

"Where does Mr. Lorenzo live?" I asked, concealing the knife in my pyjama pocket.

"Why would you want to know that now?' Laura asked, crossly.

"Just tell me," I said, indignantly.

"No. 313, 3rd Avenue, Crestwood Lane, Modena."

When we reached closer to Mr. Lorenzo's house. I revealed the identity of the killer to Laura.

"Why would you come here at this time of the day?" Laura asked, looking perplexed.

"Mr. Lorenzo is the killer, Laura," I said, bluntly.

"No way, Luca," Laura said, startled.

"He's a chain smoker, remember? He was the only one who smoked at St. Agnes. The matron doesn't smoke and neither does pastor James."

"So?" Laura asked, shrugging

"You said Giulia has cigarette burns on both of her arms. Put two and two together," I said, knocking her lightly on the head.

"Oh my God! Why didn't it strike me before?" Laura said, gasping loudly.

"We'll make him pay for what he did," I said, balling my fists.

"It's not a good idea. Let the police handle it," Laura said, rubbing my shoulder blades.

"All these years went by, and the police didn't lift a finger to look into Giulia's disappearance. Sorry if I don't trust the law anymore."

"We shouldn't take justice into our own hands," Laura said, holding my face in her hands.

"If Lorenzo goes to prison, he'll have a jolly good time there. He'll get bail in less than a day, don't you understand?

He'll never face the consequences of his actions."

"Let's just go back. Give me the knife," Laura said, reaching for the knife.

"No, I won't," I said, backing away from her.

I marched up to the main door. I rang the doorbell repeatedly and banged my fists against the door. A few seconds later, the door creaked open. Mrs. Lorenzo was cradling a baby in her arms.

"Who are you?" Mrs. Lorenzo asked, looking alarmed.

"We're from St. Agnes. We've come to see Mr. Lorenzo," I said, taking a peek inside.

"He's sleeping now. I'll let him know you dropped by when he gets up. Do you want coffee?" Mrs. Lorenzo asked with a pleasant smile.

"No, thanks. Where is his bedroom?" I asked, standing on my tippy-toes.

"The one on the far left, opposite the kitchen," Mrs. Lorenzo said, pointing to the bedroom.

Laura and I dashed to the bedroom and swung the door wide open.

"You son of a bitch! You'll pay for what you did," I said, barging inside.

"Wha-what? Who the hell are you?" Mr. Lorenzo asked, jolting awake.

I grabbed him by the collar of his shirt and pulled out the knife from my jacket.

"Oh, God! Please don't kill me. Is it money that you want? I'll give it all to you," Mr. Lorenzo said, his breath shuddering.

"I'm afraid this can't be resolved with money. Only with bloodletting," I said with a murderous glare.

"Oh, God. Don't hurt me. I have a wife and kid," Mr. Lorenzo said, tears spilling from his eyes.

"You should've thought of them before you raped and murdered that innocent girl," I said, clenching my teeth.

"Who are you talking about?" Mr. Lorenzo asked, looking confused.

"Giulia!"

"H-h-how did you know....?" Mr. Lorenzo asked, gaping at me.

"It's pretty simple, you see, Laura here has nightmares of her twin. In her nightmares, she sees Giulia wearing a white frock with blood stains and cigarette burns on both of her arms. You're the only one who smokes at St. Agnes."

"I'm really sorry for what I did. I've atoned for my sins," Mr. Lorenzo said, looking away from me.

"Oh, have you now?" I asked, scoffing.

"Yes. I'm a changed man now," Mr. Lorenzo said, taking a deep breath.

"How can you rape a little child?" I asked, catching a sob in my throat.

"I was a different man back then. A beast with perverted thoughts and uncontrollable urges, really."

"Who is to say you wouldn't rape your own daughter when she grows up to be Giulia's age," I asked, tears stinging my eyes.

"I would never hurt my baby girl," Mr. Lorenzo said, weeping bitterly.

"I'm doing this for me, Laura, and most importantly, for Giulia," I said in a somber tone.

"I'll confess my crime to the police. I'll do my time. Please don't kill me," Mr. Lorenzo said, joining his hands together.

"It's too late for that now," I said, scowling at him.

I plunged the knife into his neck. Blood squirted from his neck and sprayed all over the room.

"Rot in hell, monster!" I cried.

His wife came dashing to the room and gasped loudly.

"Ahhhhhhhh!" Mrs. Lorenzo let out a blood-curdling scream.

"Please step aside, Mrs. Lorenzo. This man deserved to die like this." I said, looking at his corpse lying in the pool of his own blood.

"I'm calling the police," Mrs. Lorenzo said, scrambling towards the bedroom door.

She locked Laura and me inside the bedroom and rushed to the living room.

"Hello, yes. There's been a murder.... My husband has been murdered!" Mrs. Lorenzo said in a trembling voice.

She gave them the address and cut the call.

A police car arrived outside the house minutes later. Blue and red lights streamed through the curtains in the bedroom, blinding me momentarily. Two burly policemen stepped inside the house. Mrs. Lorenzo led them to the bedroom and unlocked the bedroom door.

"You're under arrest for the murder of Mr. Lorenzo Giovanni. Anything you say can and will be used against you in a court of law," one of the policemen said, pinning me to the floor.

The policemen slapped handcuffs onto my wrists and escorted me out of the house. The neighbours thronged in front of the house, trying to catch a glimpse of my face.

"I love you, Laura. Promise me you'll take care of yourself while I'm away," I said, looking at her with tender affection.

"Promise. I love you more than life, Luca......." Laura said, her voice cracking.

The policemen grabbed me by the neck shoved me into the police car and drove away. Laura chased after the car till could no more. She waved at me frantically. I turned my head to wave back at her, tears rolling down my cheeks.

"He's a good man. You hear me? Leave him alone, you brutes!" Laura screamed at the top of her lungs and flailing her arms frantically.

"I'll be back soon. Stay strong for me, dear," I murmured, blowing a kiss at her through the misty police car window.

The last I saw of her before going to prison for a year was the image of her crying hysterically.

CHAPTER FIFTEEN

DOING TIME

"The LORD hears the needy and does not despise his captive people." (Psalm 69:33)

There is one and only one word to describe prison: Hell. I did nothing in my cell but read the bible and sleep. Read, sleep, repeat. The cycle continued for the rest of the year. The meal at prison mostly consisted of stale bread and slurry gravy. If you were lucky, you'd get a piece of mutton in the gravy. I share the cell with another man. He asked me why I was in prison. I told him I was in prison because I avenged my childhood friend's death. He told me he was in prison for robbing a bank. Once, a guy shivved me in the washroom. He wanted me to flash my penis so he could suck it. When I refused, he stabbed me with a shiv in the stomach. I ended up in the prison hospital for nearly two months.

I really missed Laura. I get to see her once a week during visitation hours. She came every Friday to see me. The visitation hours took place in the prison break room. We were strictly not allowed to touch or hug each other.

"Why did you kill him, Luca?" Laura asked, resting her hands under her chin.

"I couldn't help myself. I know this is not fair to you," I said, looking away from her.

"You could've let the police handle it. Look where you're at now," Laura said, scrutinizing the break room.

"I really miss you, dear," I said, slouching in my chair.

"I miss you too..." Laura's voice trailed off.

"I'll be getting out in less than six months," I said, sitting up straight.

"I know. We need to start planning our wedding," Laura said, eagerly.

"Yeah, nothing grand," I said, seeming uninterested in the wedding preparation.

"Obviously. We don't have money to throw a lavish wedding," Laura said, rolling her eyes.

"Anything interesting happening in your life?" I asked, pulling my chair forward.

"Not really. Work is boring as usual," Laura said, sulking.

"Sorry to hear that," I said, smiling wistfully.

"I live all by myself in the apartment. A really dull life I'm leading. Let me tell you that," Laura said, sighing.

"I understand," I said, feeling bad for her.

"Even though you're the one behind bars, I'm the one who feels trapped," Laura said, moping.

"You won't feel trapped for much longer. I'll be back soon, dear," I said with a glint of hope in my eyes.

"Just a week ago, four men were hitting on me at the diner," Laura said, gloomily.

"What? Are they regulars?" I asked, raising my eyebrows.

"Not really."

"What happened, dear? Tell me everything," I said, sounding troubled.

"They offered me fifty thousand euros to sleep with all of them. One man every night for four nights," Laura said, looking disgusted.

"Oh, God!" I said, gasping softly.

"I refused of course. A lotta women at the diner can't afford to pay their rent, so they would've taken up the offer in a heartbeat-"

"You're not like other women so...." I cut her off.

"The men were pretty insistent," Laura said, frowning.

"Of course, they were," I said, huffing.

"They told me they knew all about me. They knew you were in prison. They told me selling my body would be my only way out of the shithole which is my life."

"I swear to God, I'll murder them if I see them," I said, stomping my feet in rage.

"No need to worry about that," Laura said, squeezing my shoulder.

"Why?"

"They died in a fire three days ago. They all live together as bachelors in a dude cave they call home. Their house was engulfed in flames."

"Divine justice, wouldn't you say?" I asked, tipping back in my chair and whistling.

"Yeah."

"Take care, Laura," I said, smiling at her.

"I will," Laura said, smiling back at me.

"Anything else you wanna tell me?" I asked inquisitively.

"Adriana just had her baby last night," Laura said, leaning closer to me.

"How do you know that?" I asked, shocked.

"She called me on the phone this morning. She had a baby boy," Laura said, beaming like a sunflower.

"Aww! How's her boyfriend?" I asked, tilting my head.

"He's good. They're getting married soon," Laura said, dreamy-eyed.

"That's such good news, dear. I'm so happy for her," I said, rapping the table.

"She apologized to me for hitting on you," Laura said, ruffling her eyebrows.

"That happened ages ago," I said, clicking my tongue.

"I told her it was all in the past and that I was not holding it against her," Laura said with a warm smile.

"She told me it was her pregnancy hormones making her do things she wouldn't do otherwise," I said, staring into space.

"Does that mean I'll start randomly hitting on other guys when I get pregnant?" Laura asked, looking shocked.

"You better not," I said, shaking a finger at me.

"You better get your shit together and get out of this godforsaken place soon or I'm leaving you for another guy," Laura said with a smug look on her face.

"Do you really mean that?" I asked, feeling blue.

"Of course, not! Can't you take a joke?" Laura asked, slapping her forehead.

We were laughing when we heard a moaning sound coming from one of the cells.

"Give it to me, Rolando. Give it to me like that. God yes!"

"Who is that?" Laura asked, looking alarmed.

"That is Fiona. She's in the cell next to me. She murdered her husband because he cheated on her with another woman. The man she's banging right now is her neighbour, Rolando. He comes here pretty often."

"I'm sorry you've to hear that often," Laura said, cringing.

"He pays the guards a lumpsum for these conjugal visits," I said, eyeing a guard standing at the entrance of the break room.

"So, he's a rich guy then?" Laura asked, putting her hands behind the back of her head.

"Oh, yeah. Mad rich," I said, rubbing the tips of my fingers together.

"I don't want you going anywhere near Fiona. You hear me?" Laura asked, glaring at me.

"Why on earth would I do that?" I said, looking lost.

"You're one handsome fella, mister. I don't want her getting her mitts all over you," Laura said, fuming.

"Somebody's jealous, isn't she?" I asked, smirking.

"Of course, I am. I'm your fiancée for heaven's sake," Laura said, scoffing.

"You still have those night terrors?" I asked, wearing a worried expression on my face.

"Not often. It's been more than five months since I last had a night terror," Laura said, cheerily.

"That's wonderful, dear!" I said, almost jumping up for joy.

"How is that wound on your stomach?" Laura asked, eyeing my stomach.

"It's healing, but the scar looks nasty," I said, lifting my shirt to reveal the scar.

"The price you pay for not flashing your cazzo around here," Laura said, sighing.

"He didn't just wanna see it. He wanted to suck it," I said, my face turning red.

"Oh, Lordy!" Laura said, grimacing.

"There are a lotta rapists in here. Let me tell you that," I said, lowering my voice.

"Really?" Laura asked, her eyes widened.

"Uh-huh. My cellmate was raped by his former cellmate," I said, flinching.

"That's awful!" Laura let out a horrified gasp.

"I need to keep my eyes peeled around here," I said, looking around the room nervously.

"Be careful, Luca," Laura whispered.

"I will, dear," I whispered back.

"I'll get going now. My work starts in an hour," Laura said, getting up from her chair.

"Go on then. I'll see you next week," I said, waving at her.

After Laura left, I headed to my cell. On my way to my cell, I passed by Fiona's cell. She was getting plowed by her neighbour. Their pants were around their ankles.

"Join us, Luca. Let's have a threesome," Fiona called out to me from her cell.

"No, thank you," I said, covering my face with my hands.

I rushed to my cell and plopped down on my bed.

"Was it Fiona asking you for a threesome again?" Claudio asked, smirking.

"Yup."

"She's a whore," Claudio said, looking repulsed.

"I guess," I said with a shrug.

"Who did you meet today?" Claudio asked, leaning against the drywall.

"My fiancée," I said, twiddling my thumbs.

"That's nice," Claudio said, whistling. "She pretty?"

"Yeah, but if I'm being completely honest, her twin is much prettier than her," I said, blushing.

"Why don't you marry her then?" Claudio asked, scratching his head.

"She's dead, Claudio. Avenging her death is what got me in prison," I said, hurting.

"Oh, yeah. Sorry about that," Claudio said, apologetically.

"It's okay," I said with an insincere smile.

"I'm going to sleep now. Talk later?" Claudio said, getting in his bed.

"Sure. I'll just read a book," I said, picking up the book I was reading before.

I was released early from prison on account of exhibiting good behaviour during the time I spent in prison.

When I returned home from prison a year later, I was a changed man.

CHAPTER SIXTEEN

THE WEDDING DAY

"So they are no longer two, but one flesh. Therefore what God has joined together, let no one separate." (Matthew 19:6)

A week after I got out of prison, Laura and I got married. We married at a courthouse. Only Adriana, her boyfriend, and her new-born baby were present as witnesses at our wedding. I wore a crisp black suit and Laura wore a second-hand white gown she got at a thrift store. It looked so beautiful on her. It didn't seem like a second-hand gown at all.

I lifted her veil after we signed in the register and kissed her on the lips. Adriana and her boyfriend tossed some rose petals on our heads in the air to mark the occasion.

"Now you're Mrs. Laura Bianchi. How do you feel about that?" I asked, pinching her rosy cheeks.

"Fantastic! I'm the luckiest woman alive on earth," Laura said with a twinkle in her eye.

"And I'm the luckiest guy alive on earth," I said, smiling at her.

We went to a restaurant after the wedding.

"Buy anything you fancy. It's on me," I said, placing my hands on hers.

"Really?" Laura asked, unable to contain her excitement. "I'll get a chicken parm and bruschetta."

"Of course, that's what you're getting, Same old Laura," I said, grinning at her. "I'll have a Brodetto."

We ate our meal in silence and headed back to the apartment.

"I'm tired from all that standing," Laura said, stretching her legs.

"So am I," I said, stifling a yawn.

"I'm gonna go to sleep," Laura said, sauntering towards the bedroom.

"Before you go, we didn't talk about our honeymoon," I said, grabbing her arm.

"What's there to talk about it? We can't afford it, Luca," Laura said with a sad smile.

"We can if we don't spend our vacation in Bora Bora or Bali," I said, sneering.

"Okay, so which place do you have in mind?" Laura asked impatiently.

"A motel maybe," I said, tapping my middle finger on my chin.

"A motel?" Laura asked, looking astonished.

"Yeah, maybe just a night at a motel," I said with a shrug.

"Where do we have motels here in this neighbourhood?" Laura asked, grumpily.

"There's one just three blocks away from our apartment. It's called *Il Modesto*," I said, scratching the back of my neck.

"Hopefully, it's not too modest," Laura said with a nervous chuckle.

"Yeah, but it's all we can afford right now," I said, pouting.

"Can't we just spend the night here?" Laura asked, groaning.

"That would be boring, wouldn't it?" I said, lifting her chin.

"Yeah, it would," Laura said with a sullen look on her face.

"We'll have a jolly good time at the motel. Trust me," I gave her a smile of assurance.

"Yeah. I'm going to bed," Laura said, looking dejected.

"I'll join you," I said, following her to the bedroom.

We got in bed together.

"There's something you're forgetting," I said, smirking.

"What?" Laura asked, looking clueless.

"We're husband and wife now," I said, flashing her a grin.

"Yeah, so?" Laura said nonchalantly.

"We can have sex now. It won't be a sin," I said, shaking her by the shoulder gently.

"We could have sex now, but can't we save it for the night of the honeymoon?" Laura asked, linking her fingers through mine.

"Yeah, that would be so much better," I said, half-heartedly.

"I'm dying to sleep with you, but we should contain ourselves," Laura said, holding a pillow close to her chest.

"We should," I said, taking a deep breath.

"We're losing our virginities at *Il Modesto* and it's final," Laura said, looking determined.

"Looking forward to it," I said with a naughty smile.

"When should we go there?" Laura asked, resting her head on my shoulder.

"Tonight?"

"Why tonight? It's too soon," Laura said with a sudden jerk of the head.

"Tonight is the first night after our wedding. It's a special night," I said, stroking her hair.

"So, we're going there tonight?" Laura asked, fidgeting with her ring.

"Yeah. Anything you need to pack?" I said, rocking my pillow back and forth in my lap.

"Yeah, a comb, a nightdress, and maybe a toothbrush and a tube of paste," Laura said, looking around the room.

"You're forgetting something else," I said, running a hand through my hair.

"What?"

"Condoms," I said, biting my bottom lip.

"Condoms? You sure about that?" Laura asked, sounding displeased.

"Yeah, why?" I asked with a blank look on my face.

"If we're trying to make a baby, we shouldn't be using condoms," Laura said in a serious tone.

"It's too soon in the marriage to have a child, Laura," I said, placing a hand on her belly.

"I don't care. I want a child. Give me a child, Luca," Laura said, looking me straight in the eye.

"Okay then. We're not using condoms," I said, instantly regretting I'd said that.

"Yeah."

"You know we have all the time in the world to make a baby, right?" I said, caressing her cheeks.

"I know, but I don't know if I'll be fertile for long," Laura said, taking my hand away from her face.

"Why do you say that?" I asked, sounding worried.

"It's just that with you going to prison and me going to work night and day, I've been nothing but stressed. And it's not easy to have a child when you're stressed."

"I get that, but I'm not sure if I'm ready to become a father yet," I said, averting my gaze.

"Nonsense! You'll make a great dad, Laura said, nudging my arm.

"How do you know that?" I asked, narrowing my eyes.

"Look at Adriana. She didn't know the first thing about motherhood when she got pregnant. But she's a pro now."

"Yeah, you're right, I said, shaking my head.

"We're both in this together. We'll raise the child together," Laura said, squeezing my arm.

"Are you sure you're ready to be a mom?" I asked, cracking my knuckles.

"I've been ready my whole life," Laura said with confidence.

"You'll make a great mom, Laura," I said, kissing her forehead.

"Aww, thanks, dear. That means a lot," Laura said, flattered.

"I really mean it. I've seen the way you're around with kids," I said, taking her hands in mine.

"I love kids, and so does Giulia," Laura said, brooding.

"She really did love them, didn't she?" I said with a heavy heart.

"Yeah..."

"Too bad she was a kid when she died," I said with a heavy sigh.

"She never got a chance to experience motherhood," Laura said, catching a sob in her throat.

"Lorenzo robbed her of a chance to become a mother. He robbed her of life itself," I said, getting upset.

"I'll never find it in my heart to forgive him," Laura said, gritting her teeth.

"Me neither, but Christ says we must love those who sin against us," I said, rubbing her back to calm her down.

"Yes, but it's not easy," Laura said, exhaling heavily.

"I know."

"All this talk is making me woozy," Laura said, clutching her head.

"God, yes. I need to sleep," I said, my eyes drooping.

"Okay then, go to sleep. We've got a baby to make tonight," Laura said and then quietly slipped under the sheets.

CHAPTER SEVENTEEN

THE SEEDY MOTEL

"And the man and his wife were both naked and were not ashamed." (Genesis 2:25)

We arrived at the motel at ten in the night. We unpacked all our things and settled in bed. I read the Bible and Laura prayed. Laura combed her hair in front of the cracked mirror while I washed my face in the washroom.

"There's a brown sludge coming out of this tap," I said, covering my mouth with my hands.

"Eww!"

"There are also bloodstains on the wall," I said, retching.

"I'm not bathing here, and it's final," Laura said, shuddering.

"Good thing we took a good hot shower at the apartment," I said, coming out of the washroom.

We got in bed, and Laura started undressing.

"What is this on the sheets?" Laura asked, pointing at a huge stain on the sheets.

"I think it's semen..." I said, moving closer to get a better look at the stain.

"Oh, God! They haven't changed the bedsheets," Laura said, feeling sick to her stomach. "We could've just had sex in our clean and cozy bed."

"No point thinking about that now. We're already here now," I said, rubbing her back.

"Yeah, you're right," Laura said, shaking her head.

I removed my shirt and my trousers.

"Are those the branches of a tree?" I asked, looking surprised.

"What?"

"The scar you got when the matron whipped you on the back," I said, peering at her back.

"Oh yeah, it's still there," Laura said, pushing her hair aside to reveal the scar.

I kissed her lips and trailed a finger down her back.

"Luca...."

I pulled down her panties, removed her bra, and gently laid her in bed. I planted gentle kisses on her smooth belly as I went down on her.

"Oh, God!" Laura said, gasping softly.

She got on top of me and started riding me with fiery passion. I started feeling her scars.

"You're turned on by my scars?" Laura asked, panting.

"Yeah, I love them..." I said, breathing heavily.

I pinned her to the bed and sucked on her nipples tenderly.

"Your soft nipples feel so good in my mouth," I said, closing my eyes in pure bliss.

"I want you inside of me," Laura said, spreading her legs wide open.

I could see that her lady garden was well trimmed. Her lovely garden was watering just for me. I needed to deflower her and consummate our marriage.

I took her long-preserved virginity at that moment and she moaned loudly.

"Ahhh!" She screamed in excruciating pain.

"Does it hurt?" I asked, sounding worried.

"A bit, yes," Laura said, wincing.

I squeezed her twins as I continued to make love to her.

"Don't stop. Don't stop, Luca!" She screamed as she dug her nails into my skin.

I got really hard when she screamed out my name, and I came inside of her.

"How's that for a first time?" I asked, wheezing.

I rolled over to the side and slipped my arm around her waist.

"I don't wanna sleep on these semen-covered sheets, Luca," Laura said, sitting up in bed.

"I have a spare blanket. We can use the blanket to cover the stain," I said, smiling at her.

Laura and I got up from the bed. I spread the blanket over the bedsheet. Then we got back in bed.

"Come here," I said, motioning her to come closer to me.

She scooted towards me and started caressing my cheeks.

"I'm so glad we saved ourselves for tonight," Laura said, circling her finger on my nipples.

"Me too," I said, fondling her breasts under the sheets.

"What is that?" Laura asked, wrinkling her nose.

"Someone's smoking in the next room," I said, pinching my nose.

"And what is that sound?" Laura asked, covering her ears with her hands.

"Is that how you like it, bitch?" The man in the room adjacent to ours yelled out loud.

"Some man is having sex with a prostitute," I said, looking disgusted.

"I can't stay here," Laura muttered, cradling herself back and forth in bed.

"Why? What happened?" I asked, putting my arm around her.

"The smell of smoke? It's triggering me," Laura said, tears welling up in her eyes.

"Okay, we'll leave then," I said, resting her head against my chest.

"Oh my God! I can't breathe," Laura said, gasping for air.

"Hey, hey, take deep breaths. Put on your clothes. We'll leave in another five minutes," I said, lifting her chin.

"Giulia was murdered by that monster!" Laura cried as her vision blurred.

"Okay, dear. Look at me," I said, holding her face in my hands.

"She was here, Luca," Laura said, staring into my eyes.

"What?"

"She was here when we were having sex," Laura said, pointing at nothing in front of us.

"Really?" I asked, narrowing my eyes.

"She was staring at me. She looked like she wanted to kill me," Laura said, whimpering.

"She doesn't want to kill you, Laura," I said, stroking her hair.

"I'm gonna pass out, Luca," Laura said, clutching her head.

"Okay, let's just go. I packed her bag and mine and led her out of the motel. We got on a bus and reached the apartment at midnight.

"Are you okay now, dear?" I asked, laying her gently in bed.

"No," she said, shaking her head like a toddler.

I dashed to the kitchen, filled a glass of ice water, and brought it to the bedroom.

"Here, drink this," I said, handing her the glass the water.

She guzzled the water in one sip.

"I should've never married you, Luca. This is a mistake," Laura said, placing the glass on the bedside table.

"No, it's not," I said, hurting.

"I shouldn't have had sex with you. It was wrong," Laura said, looking away from me.

"There's nothing wrong about it, Laura," I said, shaking her by the shoulder.

"I've hurt Giulia. I'm no better than Mr. Lorenzo or the pastor," Laura said, sobbing.

"Look here. You did nothing, okay? Stop being so hard on yourself," I said, getting upset.

"I can't help it," Laura said, resting her head on my shoulder.

"Maybe God wanted us to marry each other and not me and Giulia. This was meant to be," I said, squeezing her arm.

"How do you know that?" Laura asked, sniveling.

"If God wanted me to marry Giulia, he would've made it happen already," I said with a sad smile.

"This doesn't feel right," Laura said, gripping her necklace.

"It's just your guilt speaking here. You feel bad you're alive and not Giulia," I said with a heavy sigh.

"Maybe," Laura said, pouting her lips.

"Just go to sleep, okay? Everything will be alright. I'm here for you," I said, pulling her close to me and cradling her in my arms like she were a small child.

CHAPTER EIGHTEEN

The Good News

"Behold, children are a gift of the LORD, The fruit of the womb is a reward." (Psalm 127:3)

A week later, our lives returned to normal. Laura and I were getting dressed to leave for work.

"What is that smell?" Laura asked, scrunching her nose.

"Milk and eggs," I said, blankly.

"I'm gonna throw up," Laura said, gagging.

"Oh, come on. Not this again," I said, slapping my forehead.

She ran to the bathroom and started barfing into the toilet bowl.

"What's going on, dear?" I asked, pulling her hair back as she continued to heave into the toilet bowl.

"I don't know," Laura said, wiping her mouth.

"You complain about the smell all the time, but this is the first time you're puking," I said, reaching my hand out for her to take it.

"I think I'm pregnant, Luca," Laura said, slowly getting up from the bathroom floor.

"No way," I said, my eyes nearly popping out of my sockets.

"We had sex recently at the motel, remember?" Laura said, her face turning red.

"Yeah, but still......" I said, biting my bottom lip.

"I'm having morning sickness. It's common among pregnant women," Laura said, rubbing her belly.

"Should we just go see a doctor?" I asked, concerned.

"No, we can't afford that," Laura said, sulking.

"Then how can we know for sure if you're pregnant?" I asked, crossly.

"Go to the store and get me a pregnancy kit," Laura said, steadying herself.

"That's a good idea. Do you need anything else?" I asked as I headed out of the bathroom.

"No, nothing else," Laura said, shaking her head.

After my shift got over, I bought the pregnancy kit. I also bought a carton of cheap chocolate milk, a few stale apples, and a box of crusty choco chip cookies.

"Any reason for buying all this? You're throwing a party?" Adriana asked, eyeing the items as she tossed them in a bag.

"I think my wife is pregnant, so I'm just getting her a couple of things she might need," I said, leaning against the counter.

"Congratulations, Luca! You're going to become a dad," Adriana said, clapping her hands together.

"I don't know if she's actually pregnant," I said with a shrug.

"She sure is. Do call me when you get the good news," Adriana said, handing me the bag.

"Sure," I said, smiling at her.

I took the items and headed to the apartment.

"I've got the pregnancy kit right here," I said, waving the pregnancy kit in front of her face.

"What are all these things?" Laura asked, eyeing the huge bag in my hand.

"You kept saying how I can buy better stuff instead of the spoilt milk, bad eggs, and the overripe bananas. So, I got some chocolate milk, stale apples, and crusty cookies."

"Why now though?" Laura asked, folding her arms across her chest.

"You might be pregnant. You need to eat well, dear," I said, emptying the contents of the bag onto the dining table.

"Aww, thanks, Luca. Didn't I tell you could buy better stuff for the same price?" Laura said, nudging his arm.

"You're always so right, dear. Remind me to never doubt you again," I said, booping her nose.

"Give me the pregnancy kit," Laura said, holding out her hand.

She took the kit and went into the bathroom. She peed on the stick and waited for five minutes.

"Are you done, dear?" I asked, knocking softly on the bathroom door.

"Yeah, just a minute, dear. The result will soon be in," Laura said, sounding angsty.

She came out of the bathroom a minute later, holding the stick in her hand.

"What does it say?" I asked, looking her in the eye.

She just stood there, looking stunned.

"Say something, dear," I said, getting worried.

"I'm pregnant, Luca!" Laura said, jumping for joy.

"Really?" I asked in disbelief.

"Yes. It shows positive, see," I said, pointing at the stick.

"What does this smiley face stand for?" I asked, scratching my head.

"If you get a smiley face, it means you're pregnant, and if you get a frowning face, it means you're not pregnant."

"That sounds rather childish," I said, chuckling.

"You got me this one. There are also kits without these faces. They just show the positive or the negative sign here."

"How do you feel?" I asked, grinning at her.

"Like I'm on top of the world," Laura said, flipping her hair back and forth.

"You're gonna be a mom, Laura!" I squealed in delight.

"And you're gonna be a dad, dear," Laura said, holding my face in her hands.

"I can't believe it," I said in a shaky voice.

"Me neither," Laura said, looking dazed.

"Let me just call Adriana," I said, pulling out my phone from my back pocket.

"Now? Why?" Laura asked with a puzzled expression.

"I promised her I'd call her if the result came in as positive," I said, shifting my weight from one foot to the other.

"Go ahead. Call her then," Laura said, placing a hand on my shoulder.

I called her on my phone. She picked up moments later.

"Hello? Is this Luca?" Adriana asked, sounding nervous.

"Yes," I said with a chuckle.

"Is she pregnant?" Adriana asked, really hoping I'd say yes.

"Yes!" I said, unable to contain my excitement.

"Can you give the phone to Laura?" Adriana asked, coyly.

"Sure," I said, enthusiastically.

I handed the phone to Laura.

"Congrats on becoming a mom," Adriana said, almost screaming into the speaker.

"Thanks."

"I'll let my boyfriend know as soon as he gets off from work. Talk to you later," Adriana said, cheerily.

"Talk to you later, Adriana," Laura said, swaying from side to side.

Laura switched off the screen and gave the phone to me.

"I'm not sure if I should have this kid, Luca," Laura said, looking away from me.

"Why?" I asked, looking muddled.

"This should be Giulia's child, not mine. She should've been the one pregnant with your child, not me."

"Oh, we're not going over this again," I said, sounding exasperated.

"We need to get rid of this baby," Laura said, catching a sob in her throat.

"We're not getting rid of this baby," I said, incensed.

"Why not?" Laura asked, scowling at me.

"We can't, Laura. It's a sin to abort a child, don't you know that? Would you want to get rid of this miracle of life that God has given us? It would be an insult to Him."

"I can't carry this child knowing that my twin is out there longing for one," Laura said, looking gloomy.

"She'll be happy for you, Laura," I said, taking her hands in mine.

"No."

"When you have a child, it's like she has one too. Remember what your mother said. Everything you feel, she feels it too," I said, lifting her chin.

"Yeah...."

"She'd want you to have this child," I said, looking her dead in the eye.

"You're sure?" Laura asked, doubtfully.

"I'm sure," I said, squeezing her shoulder.

"Guess we're having a baby then," Laura said, beaming at me.

"Do you want it to be a boy or girl?" I asked, eyeing her belly.

"I don't mind both, although a boy child would be nice," Laura said, looking down at her stomach.

"I want a girl child," I said, pinching her cheeks.

"Really?" She thought I was fibbing for a second there.

"Yes. I've always wanted to have a girl child," I said with a sparkle in my eyes.

"You're the first guy I've heard say that. My dad was very upset when my mom had female twins."

"That's sad," I said, frowning.

"He wanted at least one of the twins to be a boy," Laura said, heartbroken.

"How did he pass away?" I asked, curiosity getting the best of me.

"He died in the car crash with my mom," Laura said, averting her gaze.

"Oh, Lord. I'm sorry to hear that...."

"It's okay. He was a douchebag," Laura said, taking a deep breath.

"He sure sounds like it," I said, scoffing.

"He used to beat my mom often," Laura said, blubbering

"Oh no..."

"He never said it out loud but I knew he hated my mom and both Giulia and me," Laura said with a heavy heart.

"He deserves to go to hell," I said, gritting my teeth.

"Why did my mom have to die with him?" Laura asked, heaving a sigh.

"She didn't have to go that way," I said with a sullen look on my face.

"My dad would've been so mad at me if he found out I was having a girl baby," Laura said, sounding upset.

"Now he doesn't have to worry about that," I said, scorning.

"Sorry to interrupt, but can I drink some of this chocolate milk?" Laura asked, eyeing the carton of chocolate milk on the dining table.

"Sure. I bought it for you," I said, smiling at her.

Laura drank a glass of chocolate milk and went to bed while I went to the bathroom to take a shower.

CHAPTER NINETEEN

IN LOVE WITH THE WHITE FROCK

"Husbands, love your wives and do not be harsh with them."
(Colossians 3:19)

When I came back from work at noon, Laura was sitting in the rocking chair beside the window. She was gazing out of the window and stroking her belly. She was humming a nursery rhyme. She has a really lovely voice by the way. I bought her the rocking chair. I told her it would be good for the baby. The baby could be lulled to sleep as it listened to the humdrum of the city and the sounds of the waves lapping on the shore in the far distance.

She was wearing a maternal dress. It was a pure white frock. I was so turned on by her frock. I just stood there, stunned like a possum.

"Are you okay, baby?" Laura asked, sounding concerned.

"Yeah, I'm alright," I said with a poker face.

"What is it? You look like you got hit by a truck," Laura said, giggling.

"It's just your frock..." I said, unable to take my eyes off of her frock.

"What about it?" Laura asked, looking confused.

"You look so beautiful in that white frock," I said, whistling.

"Aww! Thanks," Laura said, blushing.

"Come here, dear," I said, beckoning her to come towards me.

She slowly got up from the rocking chair, clutching her big belly, and waddling towards me.

"Be careful, dear," I said, taking her hands in mine.

"I can't stand any longer. My feet hurt. What is it?" Laura asked, shifting her weight from one foot to the other.

"I'm so turned on by your frock," I said, feeling the fabric of her frock.

"We can't have sex now...." Laura said, taking my hand away from her dress.

"Why not?" I asked crossly.

"It'll hurt the baby," Laura said with a serious expression.

"No, it won't," I said, scoffing.

"I don't know, dear. I just want what's best for the baby," Laura said, taking a deep breath.

"I want that too, but having sex won't hurt the child. Trust me," I said, caressing her cheeks.

"Okay."

She pulled her frock over her head, unhooked her bra, and flung it on the floor.

"Your jugs look huge!" I said, ogling her breasts.

"I have to use these jugs to breastfeed our baby," Laura said, cupping her breasts with her hands.

I was overwhelmed with desire. I turned savage like a beast. I went over to her and squeezed her breasts.

"Ow! Ow! Ow!" Laura yelped like a puppy.

"What's wrong, dear?" I asked, looking startled.

"My breasts are really sore. They're very tender. Please be gentle with them," Laura said with pleading eyes.

"I will," I said, brushing aside a strand of hair from her face.

I caressed her breasts and kissed her capezzolo.

"That's so much better," Laura said, bobbing her head.

I laid her in bed and pulled down her panties. I unbuckled my pants and tossed my boxers to the floor.

"You're like a drug I can't resist," I said, growling like a wild animal.

"I can't either," Laura said in a very low voice.

We made the beast with two backs. Just as I was about to climax, Laura howled in pain.

"Please stop! Stop it, dear!" Laura screamed, gripping her legs.

"Are you okay, dear?" I asked, looking worried.

"My legs are cramping. Oh God, it hurts like hell!" Laura said, wincing.

I quickly put on my boxers and my pants and placed her legs on my lap.

"Where does it hurt?" I asked, examining her legs.

"Here," Laura said, pointing to her ankles.

I grabbed a tub of cream from the bedside table. I scooped up a dollop of cream and started massaging her ankles with my hands.

"God, that feels good!" Laura said, exhaling softly.

"I'm sorry for forcing you to have sex with me. I should've known you couldn't do it in your condition," I said, sulking.

"You didn't force me, Luca. Don't you dare say that!" Laura said, getting upset.

"You did say you didn't want to have sex with me," I said, looking away from her.

"I said it because I thought it'd hurt the baby, but turns out it hurt me instead," Laura said, smiling wistfully.

"Do you want anything to eat?" I asked, getting up from the bed.

"I'll have an omelet," Laura said, rubbing her belly in circles.

"Okay. Anything you want, dear. You just lie here while I go make it," I said with a warm smile.

I went to the kitchen and prepared a Frittata instead. The mother of my child deserves nothing but the best. After I made it, I put it on a plate and took it to the bedroom along with a glass of cold apple juice.

"What is this fancy breakfast?" Laura asked, gingerly sitting up in bed.

"Consider this my meal of apology," I said, handing the plate of Frittata and the glass of apple juice to her.

"You don't have to apologize. You hear me?" Laura asked, tugging at my earlobes.

"Yes."

"Is this a Frittata?" Laura asked, her stomach rumbling.

"Uh-huh."

"She took a bite of the Frittata and moaned loudly.

"Oh, God! This is so gooood!" Laura spoke with her mouth full.

"You didn't moan so much when we had sex," I said, shaking my head.

"Food is better than sex," Laura said as continued to wolf down the omelet.

"Hey, take that back," I said, jabbing her in the ribs.

"No, I won't. Ask any pregnant woman in the world and she'll say the same thing." Laura said, putting her left hand over her mouth.

"I'll take your word for it," I said with a shrug.

"This is cheesy, creamy yet spicy. How is that possible?" Laura asked, savouring the omelet.

"It's my magic. Aren't I a good cook?" I asked with my hands behind my back.

"Yes. You're the best cook I know," Laura said, beaming at me.

"Really?" I asked, raising my eyebrows.

"Yes, of course!" Laura said, nodding her head.

"Hey, I could get used to this You should get pregnant more often," I said with a naughty smile.

"No way. One is more than enough," Laura said with a heavy sigh.

"I agree," I said with a straight face.

"That being said, I'm not entirely against the idea of having more kids," Laura said, turning to face me.

"Not anytime soon at least," I said, really hoping she wouldn't disagree.

"Definitely," Laura muttered as she gulped down the apple juice.

"You wanna sleep now?" I asked, lifting her chin.

"No, let's watch that show *La Poivre*. We haven't finished watching that," Laura said with a pouty face.

"Sure. Let's watch that," I said, smiling at her.

I turned on the TV. We plopped down on the couch and watched the show together. Halfway through the show, Laura dozed off on the couch.

"This show's really good, right?" I asked, tapping her on the shoulder.

I turned to face her and she was sleeping on my shoulder peacefully.

"What will I do with you, Mrs. Laura Bianchi?" I said, stroking her hair.

I carried her in my arms and took her to the bedroom. I tucked her up in bed, kissed her on the forehead, and tiptoed to the living room to watch the rest of the show.

CHAPTER TWENTY

GIULIA JR. (FOUR MONTHS LATER)

"You shall not make any cuttings in your flesh, for the dead, neither shall you make in yourselves any figures or marks." *(Leviticus 19:28)*

Laura started to show as the months passed by. Her baby bump was very visible now. She floated around the house like a ghost.

"Laura, are you ready, dear?" I called out to her from the living room.

"Yes, just a minute," she replied from the bedroom.

She waddled towards me Her face was glowing.

"How are you feeling?" I asked, holding out both of my arms.

"Not bad," Laura said, wrapping her arms around me.

"How's the little fella feeling?" I asked, pressing my ear against her belly.

I stroked her belly and suddenly felt a kick.

"The baby just kicked!" Laura squealed with a sparkle in her eyes.

"Really? Is that what it was?" I asked, looking up at her.

"Yes," Laura said, shaking her head.

I felt her belly and the baby kicked again.

"Someone's ready to come out of mommy's tummy," I said, kissing her baby bump.

I led Laura out of the apartment. We boarded a bus to a nearby hospital.

"Are you ready to see your baby?" The doctor asked, smiling at us.

"Yes," I responded restlessly.

The doctor lifted her maternal gown and applied a cold gel to her underbelly.

"There's the baby," the doctor said, pointing at the ultrasound of the baby.

"Aww! Look at him, Luca!" Laura said, tears filling her eyes.

"The baby is looking good. It has a healthy heartbeat. It's having a blast in your belly, ma'am."

"I hope so," Laura said, looking down at her enormous belly.

"Do you wanna know the gender of the child?" The doctor asked, removing the gloves from her hands.

"Yes, doc," Laura said with eager eyes.

"I could just write it on a piece of paper and hand it in an envelope to you. You can open it later when you're throwing a gender reveal party. It'll be a surprise."

"We're not throwing a gender reveal party. We'd like to know the baby's gender now," I said, placing a hand on Laura's shoulder.

"You're having a girl child," the doctor said with a big grin on her face.

"A girl?" Laura asked, looking disappointed.

"Yes. It's a she," the doctor, nodding her head.

"Oh my God! Yes!" I shouted, jumping for joy.

"Aren't you happy, miss?" The doctor asked, looking concerned.

"I am, it's just I wished it were a boy...." Laura said with a half-smile.

"Having girl children is so much better than having boy children. Trust me," the doctor said, squeezing her shoulder.

"Didn't I say the same thing, Laura? We're fortunate to be having a girl baby," I said, eyeing her belly.

"I guess..." Laura said, heaving a sigh.

"Have you thought of a name for the child?" The doctor asked, facing us.

"No-" I said and was soon cut off by Laura.

"Yes," Laura said quickly.

"What's the name?" The doctor asked probingly.

"Giulia," Laura said with a somber expression.

"Giulia?" The doctor asked, raising her eyebrows.

"Uh-huh. That was the name of my twin sister," Laura said, looking unfocused.

"That's a really beautiful name, miss. Where is Giulia now?" The doctor asked, peeking outside the room.

"Six feet under," Laura said, biting her bottom lip.

"Huh?" The doctor uttered.

"She's dead," Laura said, bluntly.

"Oh, oh.... I'm sorry for asking you that," the doctor said with remorse.

"It's okay. It is what it is," Laura said, misty-eyed.

"So, this is to honour her then?" The doctor asked, wiping the cold gel on Laura's underbelly with a tissue.

"Yes."

"That's wonderful," the doctor said and gave her a pat on the back.

"Before we leave, I need to ask you something, doc," I asked, moving closer to the doctor.

"What is it?" The doctor asked, turning towards me.

"Is it okay if my wife has sex with me when she's pregnant?" I asked, my face turning red.

"Yes, of course," the doctor said with a bright smile.

"Thank goodness!" I said, joining my hands together.

"Although it's likely her legs may cramp up and she may not enjoy the sex as much."

"Noted," I said with a slight nod.

"Okay then," the doctor said, reaching her hand for the doorknob.

"Thanks, doc!" Laura said as her eyes lit up.

"You're welcome, dear," the doctor replied, beaming at her.

We left the hospital and reached the apartment at noon.

"You didn't tell me you're naming the baby Giulia," I said, folding my arms across my chest.

"What other name will I give her?" Laura asked with a shrug.

"I'm more than okay with you naming the baby after your twin sister. It's just you should let me know before you make such important decisions."

"I'm sorry, Luca. It must've slipped my mind..." Laura said, looking downcast.

"It's alright, dear," I said, rubbing her back.

"I'm dead tired," Laura said, stifling a yawn.

"You wanna sleep?" I asked, yawning.

"Yes."

"I'll be in the living room then," I said, heading to the bedroom door.

"No, don't go. Stay with me," Laura said, grabbing my arm.

"Okay."

I got in bed with her and spooned her.

"Are you feeling cold?" I asked, pressing my legs against hers.

"Not anymore. Your hands and feet are really warm," Laura said, taking my hand in hers.

"It is. Your hands are really cold though," I said, shuddering.

"I can't believe I'm pregnant," Laura said, blinking her eyes.

"Me neither," I said, breathing down her neck.

"It feels like yesterday when we were fooling around outside the chapel," Laura said, lost in thought.

"I know, right?"

"Time really does fly, doesn't it?" Laura asked, exhaling softly.

"It does."

"Now we're gonna become mother and father," Laura said in disbelief.

"It's too much to digest," I said, gulping.

"Now I'm thinking we should've used protection back at the motel," Laura said, sulking.

"You were the one who said we shouldn't use condoms," I said, crossly.

"I know, but it doesn't sound so much like a bad idea right about now," Laura said, sighing.

"But it would've made the sex less pleasurable," I said, frowning.

"Really?"

"Yes. It feels better to have sex without protection," I said with a sunny smile.

"Maybe."

"Get some rest, dear. You need loads of it," I said, running my fingers through her hair.

"I know."

I waited until Laura fell asleep before sneaking into the kitchen and grabbing a glass on the counter. I dropped it to the floor and watched it shatter into a million little pieces. I grabbed a tiny shard of glass and slashed my right wrist.

"Oh, God. Please have mercy on me," I said, wailing aloud.

I didn't know how I was gonna provide for Laura and the baby. I resorted to self-harm to numb the pain I was feeling. It was easier to endure the pain inflicted on my body than the one inflicted on my heart.

"I need to stop the bleeding," I said, gripping my right wrist.

I went to the washroom and placed gauze on my wrist. Drops of blood dripped from my wrist and swirled down the sink.

"I shouldn't be doing this. It's not fair to Laura or the child. The baby needs her father," I said, staring at my reflection in the bathroom mirror.

I washed my wound with cold water and bandaged it. I tiptoed towards the bed and slipped under the sheets.

"Where did you go?" Laura asked, narrowing her eyes.

"Nowhere," I mumbled.

"Why are you lying? I saw you sneaking out of the bedroom," Laura said indignantly.

"I just went to the kitchen to drink water," I muttered under my breath.

"What's that on your wrist?" Laura asked, staring at my bandaged wrist.

"Ah, this. I accidentally slashed my right wrist with a knife while cutting an apple this morning," I said, hiding my arms behind my back.

"Oh, no! Are you okay?" Laura asked, looking alarmed.

"Yeah, I'm fine," I said, fighting back my tears.

Laura planted a gentle kiss on my right wrist and pressed it against her chest.

"Don't go around getting hurt, Luca. Our baby and I need you," Laura said, placing my hand on her baby bump.

"I know," I said, my voice cracking like shards of glass.

I made up my mind then and there I wasn't gonna hurt myself no matter how bad the situation got. I'd just have to suck it up and work harder to give what's best for my wife and my child.

Part Three (Giulia Moretti's Spirit)

CHAPTER TWENTY-ONE

CONFINEMENT

"All go to the same place; all come from dust, and to dust all return." (Ecclesiastes 3:20)

My anima is indefinitely tied to this place. This is where I was murdered, and this is my home. I can never abandon this place until my soul rests in peace.

I can't stand this place! I have nothing to do here. Luca and Laura left this place when they turned eighteen. I hate that they get to go places, and I'm stuck here.

I walk by the place my body was dumped on the night I was murdered. It's the dump yard where the kitten was killed and thrown into a gunny bag. I was dumped in a sack. Guess the kitten and I are not that different. I can still smell the kitty and my flesh rotting in the gunny bag and the sack. We were killed and thrown away like we were nothing.

I often play with the other kittens Laura and Luca had saved from Marco. They're a lovely bunch.

I was there the day the matron whipped Laura to death. I thought it was completely uncalled for. She had done nothing but save a bunch of helpless kittens. Yet, that Marco guy gets to walk free after murdering a kitten.

Her body was covered in bruises and scars. I consoled her when she ran from the children's home and came to seek solace at the chapel. It is true. I'm a ghost, and I'm very much here. But no one can see me except Laura. Luca thinks Laura is nuts. I know it. Not many men his age believe in ghosts, but ghosts do exist. It's not a lie.

I don't have a body but I have a mind. She can speak to me, but I can't speak to her. Laura can't feel me, but she can see me. It hurts that I can't speak to my one and only sister.

I have no clue how I got into this position. One minute I'm laughing at the dining table with my friends, and the next minute I'm murdered and l float around the estate as a ghost.

It didn't feel like I was killed. I lost consciousness and when I opened my eyes, I was still there, not as a human, but as a ghost. It's all so surreal.

Laura was the only one who guessed I was dead. Everyone else, but Laura and Luca, thought I ran away with that stupid gardener. They know me too well to fall for those lies.

I can't believe everyone at St. Agnes believed the horrible story that the matron weaved. The matron told Laura that she caught me having sex with the gardener. That's very funny because I've never had sex with anyone let alone with a gardener.

Now everyone thinks I'm this slut who spreads her legs for anyone. Everyone at St. Agnes hates me, and I hate them. I only like Laura and Luca.

St. Agnes is hell on earth and that is neither an overstatement nor an understatement. Everyone here has secrets to hide, and I know each and every one of them.

Laura was right when she guessed that the matron was screwing the pastor. They screw each other sometimes, and I've seen it. It's despicable.

One day, the matron asked the cook to leave the kitchen when the pastor came over to the children's home to have lunch. She told the cook she'd prepare lunch that day. When the cook left as per the matron's order, the matron called the pastor to the kitchen.

She removed her maroon gown, flung her panties to the floor, and sat on the counter with her legs wide open. The pastor grunted and pounced at her. They were screwing each other like wild animals.

I couldn't stand to see it anymore. The matron was supposed to cook lunch and there she was having the time of her with the pastor. I knew I had to do something to stop it. I picked up a few dishes and dropped them on the floor. The dishes clattered and smashed into a million little pieces. The cook came running to the kitchen and she saw them on the counter. The matron's legs were wrapped around the pastor's waist. The pastor's pants were around his ankles.

"What are you doing, Miss Maria?" The cook asked, her mouth wide open.

"Get out now!" The matron screamed.

"Why are you having sex with pastor James?" The cook asked, shifting her gaze from the matron to the pastor.

"I can do whatever I want," the matron said, scowling at her.

"No, you can't. Don't you know it's a sin against the Lord?" The cook said, glowering.

"I know that," the matron said, gritting her teeth.

"Then, why are you still doing it?" The cook asked, looking disappointed.

"Shut your mouth and leave," the matron said, banging her fists on the counter.

"I'll report you to the owner," the cook said, shaking her finger at the matron.

"You're going to report me to Mr. Lorenzo?" The matron asked, scoffing.

"Yes."

"Then I'll report to the owner about how you had a child out of wedlock," the matron said, sneering.

"How do you know that?" The cook asked, taken aback by shock.

"What do you mean?" The matron asked, blinking her eyes.

"I told that to pastor James in confidence during one of our confession sessions," the cook said, feeling betrayed.

"He told me," the matron said with a smug smile.

"How dare you! I trusted you, pastor James," the cook said as her eyes swelled with tears.

"You think I care about a no-nothing like you?" The pastor said, tsking.

"Go ahead and report us to the matron. Let me see you try," the matron said, folding her arms.

"I hate you, Miss Maria, and pastor James," the cook said, sniffling.

"Like we ever liked you in the first place," the matron said, cackling like a witch.

She fled the kitchen in tears. Later, Miss Maria prepared a beef noodle soup and apple pie for the children. Rudolfo slurped the beef noodle soup in one sip and gobbled down the pie in one bite.

Later that day, Laura and Luca went to the gardener's house. I was there then.

It was true the gardener had given me a white rose. I was upset that day. The pastor had asked me to give him one of my soiled panties. I didn't understand what use a pastor had with a little girl's underwear. I still gave it to him anyway.

"Why are you upset, little girl?" The gardener asked, pinching my cheeks.

"Oh, it's nothing," I said, looking gloomy.

"Here, have this white rose," the gardener said, handing me a white rose.

"Thanks, I love white roses!" I said, holding the white rose close to my chest.

"I know, dear," the gardener said, tousling my hair.

The matron came to the garden just then. She was spying on us in the distance.

"You're not allowed to pluck flowers. Don't you know that?" The matron said in a stern voice.

"I know but…" The gardener said, looking down at the ground.

"No buts," the matron said, wagging a finger in front of the gardener's face.

"Okay. I'm sorry, Miss Maria," the gardener said, moping.

"If you keep this up. I'll have to fire you, Edoardo," the matron said, looking him dead in the eye.

"Please don't." The gardener begged her.

"Then don't pluck the flowers in the garden!" The matron said, pointing at the white rose in my hand.

"I won't, Miss Maria," the gardener said, shaking his head.

"Come inside, Giulia," the matron said, beckoning me to come inside.

"Yes," I said with my hands behind my back.

I later went to Miss Maria's office that day. She was talking to Mr. Lorenzo on the phone.

"I need to tell you something, Miss Maria," I said, stepping inside her office.

"Can't it wait?" The matron asked, looking annoyed.

"No, it can't," I said, fidgeting with my necklace.

"I'll talk to you later, sir," the matron said in a very low voice.

She cut the call and faced me.

"What is so important that you've to come to my office to talk about it?" The matron asked, tapping her sharp fingernails on the desk.

"It's about the pastor," I said, blankly.

"The pastor? Pastor James?" The matron asked, raising her eyebrows.

"Yes...."

"What about him?" The matron asked, frowning.

"He took my underwear," I said, looking away from her.

"He took your underwear?" The matron asked in disbelief.

"Yes."

"Lying doesn't suit you, dear," the matron said, clicking her tongue.

"I'm not lying, Miss Maria!" I said, raising my voice.

"Yes, you are. He's a man of the cloth. He definitely wouldn't do something like that."

"But he did," I said, tears welling up in my eyes.

"No, he didn't. And if you open your mouth one more time, I'll chop off your tongue," the matron said, grimacing.

"But...."

"I had to end the call with the owner for this. What a waste!" The matron said, sighing.

I left the office, sobbing. She didn't believe the pastor took my underwear. I couldn't believe it myself. Who would believe me?

I took the white rose to my bedroom. I plucked the petals and tossed them on my bed.

I hated the matron. I wanted to burn her alive. Both Laura and I couldn't stand the matron. Neither did Luca. She was the devil in disguise.

She had this holier-than-thou attitude. She preached about chastity, but she was never chaste herself.

She knew pastor James had an underwear fetish. She just didn't want to admit it.

"Giulia, are you okay?" Luca asked, peeking inside my bedroom.

"Yes...."

"Are you sure?" Luca asked, sounding worried.

"Yes, I'm more than okay," I said, wiping my tears with the back of my hand.

"Okay, whatever you say. Laura and I are going to play in the garden. Are you coming?"

"Nope," I said, pouting.

"See you later then," Luca said, trotting outside my bedroom.

"See you later," I muttered under my breath.

I screamed and banged the door shut soon after he left.

Why was I the one who always had to suffer?

CHAPTER TWENTY-TWO

JEALOUSY

"Anger is cruel and fury overwhelming, but who can stand before jealousy?" (Proverbs 27:4)

I'm jealous of Laura. There I said it. I hate that Luca has fallen in love with her. Luca should've confessed his love to me, and not to her. He should've married me, not her. He should've gone to that seedy motel with me, and not with her. He should've had sex with me, and not with her. He should've had a baby with me, and not with her!

It's not fair that Laura gets to carry Luca's baby. What I wouldn't do to carry his child. Sometimes, I imagine ripping open Laura's belly, grabbing her fetus, and putting it inside my stomach. I want to feel what it's like to be pregnant. I want to know what it's like to get all that love and attention Laura's been getting ever since she got pregnant.

When I see Luca kissing her baby bump, I turn sick with envy. One day, Luca was stroking Laura's belly when he felt the baby kick. That was such a wholesome moment. Later, Luca made Laura a Frittata and a glass of apple juice. He always wants what's best for the mother of his child.

If I were pregnant with his child, Luca would make delicious food for me too. He would treat me like a queen. I know it. He chose me over Laura after all.

I've secretly wanted Laura to have a miscarriage. I wanted her to suffer, but not anymore. I thought if maybe she had a miscarriage, then Luca may no longer love her. He may even begin to hate her.

When she was coming out of the bathroom once after taking a shower, I made her trip and fall. She fell and lay there on the bathroom floor, whimpering. She couldn't get up because she was six months pregnant at the time.

Luca found her lying naked on the bathroom floor when he came back from work. He wrapped her in a blanket, carried her in his arms, and gently laid her in bed. Then he massaged her legs and sang lullabies to lull her to sleep. Then a horrifying thought occurred to me. If Laura had a miscarriage, Luca would love her only more. The pain of losing their child would only bring them closer together. They would mourn the loss of their child together.

Luca has never once cheated on Laura. I thought he would cheat on her with Adriana for sure. Adriana is a very pretty girl and she has a crush on him. But Luca has never made a move on her.

I don't understand what he sees in Laura. She isn't even as pretty as me, and she knows that. I think Luca feels sorry for her. All the sex he has with her is probably sympathy sex. He did fall in love with her after I went missing. He first caught feelings for her after the matron whipped her. He feels he has to look out for her and be her saviour.

I wouldn't have minded if Laura had fallen in love with Rudolfo or any other boy at St. Agnes, but she had to fall in love with my man. She's been using me as an excuse to get closer to him.

I wish I didn't die so soon. I could've married Luca, the love of my life, had his babies, and grown old with him.

I remember the night Luca first fell in love with her. It was lust rather than love. She was lying semi-conscious on the pastor's bed without a bra. She turned to the other side, and Luca saw her bare breasts for the first time. He got a massive boner right away. Luca is a man of self-control. He controlled his sexual urges and went to bed whimpering like a puppy.

I can't blame Laura for what happened. She didn't know she was topless. But she had bewitched him with her body. What Luca had with me was love, what Luca has with Laura is lust.

Then, Laura masturbated two days later. She thought of MY MAN as she touched herself. That was the last straw. I couldn't stand it any longer. I entered her bedroom and strangled her till she was blue in the face. I could've killed her, but I didn't.

She was rubbing it in my face that she could do anything she wanted with him, and I couldn't. She was falling for him. She fell hard for him the day he showed her the pornographic image of a man and a woman having sex. It all started because of the matron. If the matron had just told Laura what sex was without being vague about it, Laura and Luca wouldn't have been a thing.

I've wanted Laura and Luca to separate for a while now. But now with a baby on the way, it's never gonna happen. I hate myself for being so jealous of them and the life they've built together, but I can't help it.

When Luca said Laura and him were meant to be together, I wanted to strangle him to death. He said if God wanted me and him to be together, he would've made it happen by now.

If the tables turned, I wonder how Laura would react. If I stole her man, had sex with him, and had his baby, how would she feel?

Laura could've used protection when she had sex with Luca back at the motel. Luca even insisted they use protection, but she didn't want to use condoms She wanted to get pregnant because she was afraid of losing him. She knew the only way she could tie him to her forever was by having his child.

She knows Luca might not be faithful to her for long. Once she has his child and her boobs begin to sag and she is no longer attractive to him, he would leave her for another woman. That is exactly why I said their marriage is based on lust and not love.

Laura and Luca got married so soon because they wanted to have sex. They said so themselves. They made out and touched each other in the shower before coming to the decision to get married.

He got her a Sapphire ring right after that. I hate blue, but my sister is crazy about blue. If I were in her place, I'd want him to get me a diamond or pearl ring. Nothing more, nothing less.

And Laura is the most ungrateful girl I've ever seen! She tossed the bananas and the eggs that Luca had bought for her with his hard-earned money in the trash and she poured her glass of milk into the sink. And I don't think that was unintentional. She knows I love anything white, so by pouring the milk down the sink, she was erasing me out of her mind. She was smiling at my misery.

She was glad I was out of her life. I would no longer get in the way of her and Luca.

I am jealous of her, and she is jealous of me.

When Luca and Laura were having sex at the motel, I was closely watching them. Laura saw me and she froze in horror. I was supposed to be the one in that bed consummating my marriage with Luca.

It was true what Laura said to Luca. When Luca had sex with her, he saw me in her. The reason he was so turned on by the maternal dress that Laura was wearing was that he immediately thought of me when he saw her in that white frock.

Of course, he wouldn't admit it, but that was the truth. He was and will never be attracted to her as long as I'm stuck in his head.

When he saw her pregnant in that white frock, he wanted to have sex with her, but in actuality, he wanted to have sex with me. In his mind, I was the one carrying his baby, not Laura.

It was very funny when Laura cramped her legs while having sex with Luca. She couldn't move an inch after that. She deserved it for thinking she could still screw him with her big belly. But of course, that only made him love her even more.

I get annoyed every time Luca calls Laura "Mrs. Laura Bianchi." Bianchi is his family name, and now she's part of his family. It should've been Mrs. Giulia Bianchi, not Mrs. Laura Bianchi.

Now Laura wants to name her child after me. I don't even know why she bothers with that after everything she's done to me. She is living the life I should've lived if I were alive.

Sometimes I wish she were killed instead of me. Why does she get to live and I don't? How is God fair in doing so? He chose Laura over me the way He chose Abel's offering over Cain's.

I don't know if I'll ever find it in my heart to forgive Laura for stealing my man and having his baby.

I neither feel hatred for her nor do I wish ill for her. The only thing I feel when I think of her is a seething, gnawing and all-consuming jealousy.

173

CHAPTER TWENTY-THREE

VENGEANCE

"Since indeed God considers it just to repay with affliction those who afflict you." (2 Thessalonians 1:6)

Much like Luca, I take justice into my own hands. I have been wronged my whole life. Now, as a ghost, I get to exact my vengeance on all those who wronged me and my loved ones.

My first target was Marco, the boy who killed the kitten. He had tortured that poor kitten and he enjoyed it. As Luca said, he was going to grow up to become a serial killer, and I had to stop him.

One day, Marco was playing in the garden when he spotted the kittens. He leered at them and went inside the children's home. Later that night, he came back again, but this time with a knife. He was going to kill the rest of the kittens.

"Come to papa so you can meet your mama," he kept saying that eerie line over and over again. It was chilling to say the least.

That was when Laura and Luca spotted him waving a knife at the kittens. Laura slashed Marco's thighs with the knife. He hobbled away to the children's home, clutching his thighs.

He was planning to kill the kittens the next night. He tossed and turned in bed making plans to kill the kittens.

I entered his room and wrapped my hands around his throat.

"Hey, who is that?" Marco shouted, darting his eyes around the room.

I grabbed him by the collar and shoved him to the bedroom floor.

"Who the hell are you? Show yourself," Marco said, backing into the wall.

I pressed my hands on his stab wounds. He started yelping like a dog.

"Please don't hurt me," Marco said, getting on his knees.

I slapped him across the face and strangled him.

"Stop it. Stop it I said," Marco said, his voice cracking.

I finally let him go in peace. He ran to the matron later that night, wailing.

"Miss Maria, there's a ghost in my room," Marco said, bawling like a baby.

"What nonsense! There's no such thing as ghosts," the matron said, scoffing. "Oh, God. How did you get those stab wounds on your thighs?"

"Laura stabbed me with a knife," Marco said between sobs and sniffles.

"What?"

"They tried to kill me because I was hurting the kittens," Marca said, wiping his tears with the back of his hand.

"Why would you hurt the kittens, Marco?" The matron asked, frowning.

"I don't know. I like it I guess," Marco said with a shrug.

"Hurting animals is one thing, but hurting a human. Now that's a sin," the matron said, clicking her tongue.

"They might keep the kitties in their bedroom. I overheard them say that," Marco said, blubbering.

"Go to your bedroom, Marco. You haven't heard the last of me, mister," the matron said, shaking a finger at him.

Marco snitched on Laura and Luca to the matron. That's how the matron knew Laura was hiding the kittens in her bedroom.

I had fun hurting Marco. He had it coming. He hasn't gone near the kittens after that incident.

My second target was the pastor. I still wasn't over the fact that he had taken my underwear. He spent many nights sniffing my ripe underwear. It made me sick to my stomach.

One night when he was lying in his bed sniffing my underwear, he started coughing violently. He ran to the toilet and started coughing up blood. He spat the blood into the sink and stared in the bathroom mirror. His mouth tasted like metal. His teeth were stained with blood.

He ran to the children's home, panting. He swung open the matron's office.

"Miss Maria, I need to have a word with you," the pastor said, catching his breath.

"What is it? You can't just barge in here whenever you feel like it," the matron said, sounding alarmed.

"I'm coughing up blood, Miss Maria," the pastor said between a fit of violent coughs.

"What?" Miss Maria couldn't believe what she was hearing.

"Hand me a handkerchief," the pastor said, holding out his hand.

"Okay."

The matron grabbed a handkerchief tucked in one of her sleeves and handed it to the pastor. He coughed into the handkerchief. There was a splatter of blood on it.

"Oh no, you might be sick, pastor James," the matron said, staring at the bloody handkerchief.

"I'm paying for my sins. I should never have slept with you," the pastor said, moping.

"That's not it, pastor. You know that as well as I do," the matron said, holding his face in her hands.

The pastor coughed into the handkerchief till it was entirely covered in blood.

"Oh, God. Please have mercy on pastor James," the matron said, embracing him in her arms.

"Miss Maria, I might die anytime soon," the pastor said with a weak smile.

"Nonsense! Don't you dare say that!" The matron said, tears stinging her eyes.

The pastor was later diagnosed with lung cancer.

My third target was Miss Maria. She was by far the worst of the lot. She not only wronged me, but she also wronged my sister. She needed to pay the price.

Her chest felt very heavy and sore as the days went by. This happened after Laura and Luca had left the children's home. The matron started feeling sick often.

She went to the parsonage one night. She knocked on the door and it opened right away.

"I need to have a word with you," the matron said in a serious tone.

"What about?" The pastor asked, blinking his eyes.

"Can I come in?" The matron asked impatiently.

"Sure."

He led her to the living room. She sat on a sofa and the pastor sat on the sofa opposite her.

"What do you want to talk about?" The pastor asked, resting his hands on his lap.

"I think I might be pregnant with your child, pastor James," the matron said, twiddling her thumbs.

"Are you kidding me right now?" The pastor asked, his eyes bulging like a bulldog's.

"No, I'm not," the matron said, shaking her head.

"Why do you think you're pregnant?" The pastor asked, narrowing his eyes.

"My breasts have been feeling rather sore and tender lately," the matron said, cupping her breasts with her hands.

"So?"

"That's one of the symptoms of pregnancy," the matron said, looking him straight in the eye.

"It could be anything," the pastor said, shrugging.

"No," the matron said, biting her bottom lip.

"It's been over a year since we last had sex. There's no way you're pregnant."

"Are you sure?" The matron asked, raising her eyebrows.

"I'm sure," the pastor said reassuringly.

"Then what could this be?" The matron asked with a puzzled expression.

"I don't know. You've to take it up with a doctor. It could be serious," the pastor said, sounding worried.

"Yeah, you're right. I'll get going then," the matron said, getting up from the sofa.

"Okay then. Take care," the pastor said, smiling at her.

"Good night, pastor James," the matron said, waving at him.

"Good night, Miss Maria," the pastor said, waving back at her.

The matron was later diagnosed with breast cancer.

My fourth and final targets were the four men who harassed Laura at the diner where she works.

Laura was bending over backward to make ends meet. With her fiancé away in prison, she had to work for both of them to pay their rent.

One of the fellow waitresses told the four men where her fiancé was when they paid her a huge sum of money. That's when they started hitting on her.

"Hey, beautiful. Come here," Man 1 said, beckoning her to come towards him.

"Welcome to Donatella's diner. How may I take your order?" Laura asked, clutching her notepad.

"We'll have four grilled cheese sandwiches, please," Man 2 said, sizing her up.

"Sure. Four grilled cheese sandwiches coming right up," Laura said, turning to go.

"Hey, where are you going? We need to talk, miss," Man 1 said, grabbing her arm.

"What about? Do I know you?" Laura asked, staring at the four men.

"No, but we know where your fiancé is," Man 2 said, grinning at her.

"Really?" Laura asked, raising her eyebrows.

"Yes, and there's a way for you to pay your rent without having to slog so much," Man 1 said, squeezing her arm.

"What's a pretty woman like yourself doing in this dumpster of a diner?" Man 4 said, clicking his tongue.

"What should I do?" Laura asked, looking interested.

"You just have to sleep with each of us for four nights. We'll pay you well," Man 2 said, rubbing the tips of his fingers.

"I would never sleep with any of you. Never! My body is only for my fiancé to touch," Laura said, looking upset.

"You're walking away from 50,000 euros. Don't forget that," Man 3 said, shaking a finger at her.

"No amount of money is worth cheating on my fiancé with," Laura said, glaring at him.

"You have to do what it takes to make it in this cruel world. This is your only way to crawl out of the shithole that is your life," Man 3 said, looking at her with pity.

"I won't sleep with you all, and that's final," Laura said, stomping her feet in fury.

"You're gonna regret this, miss," Man 1 said, clenching his teeth.

"Do you still want your grilled sandwiches?" Laura asked snappishly.

"You can take those grilled cheese sandwiches and shove them up your ass. We don't want them," Man 2 said, scowling at her.

The men walked out of the diner, scorning.

"What was all that commotion about?" The fellow waitress said, rushing towards her.

"Nothing," Laura said, looking away from her.

After she finished her shift, she took a bus straight to her apartment and ran to her bedroom, weeping.

"When are you coming back, Luca? I miss you so much," Laura said, covering her face with a pillow.

I felt so bad for Laura. She shouldn't have to put up with that. I needed to make those men pay for what they did. I went over to their house at midnight. They were smoking cigars.

"That girl didn't budge, did she?" Man 1 said, blowing a cloud of smoke in the air.

"No," Man 2 said, sounding annoyed.

"She loves her fiancé way too much," Man 3 said, huffing.

"I say we kill her fiancé," Man 2 suggested, smashing his fist into his palm.

"How do we do that?" Man 4 asked, scratching his head.

"A cousin of mine is in that same prison where her fiancé is held. He'd know this fiancé of hers. One word and he'll shiv the guy," Man 2 said, leering.

That was how Luca got shivved in the washroom. It was all planned. Luckily, Luca survived that ordeal.

I had had it with those men. I went to their kitchen, grabbed a matchbox lying on the counter, started a fire, and tossed the matchstick at one of the drapes in the kitchen.

"You smell that?" Man 4 said, sniffing.

"Yes. It smells like something's burning," Man 1 said, sweating bullets.

Soon the entire house caught on fire.

"Call the fire department. Quick!" Man 2 said, jumping up and down.

I took all of their phones, cellphones, and telephones, and dumped them in front of their house. They couldn't leave the house without getting burned.

"We're gonna die!" Man 3 said, grasping the ends of his scorched hair.

After a few minutes, they all roasted in the fire. It was there in the next day's news.

"Divine justice' is what Luca called it, but it was actually my justice. Giulia's justice.

I made each and every person who wronged my sister and I pay, except for Mr. Lorenzo, because Luca took care of him for me.

CHAPTER TWENTY-FOUR

KARMA

"As I have observed, those who plow evil and those who sow trouble reap it." (Job 4:8)

Laura and Luca went to the children's home when they heard that the matron had breast cancer. Rudolfo called them and let them know. He was the only other decent guy at St. Agnes apart from Luca.

"How do you think she'd react if she saw us?" Laura asked, sounding tense.

"Probably pleased. We were the troublemakers there, after all. She'd be flattered that we came all the way from Modena to meet her."

"You're right," Laura said with a slight nod of the head.

"I'm not surprised she got breast cancer. It's karma for making our lives hell," Luca said, gritting his teeth.

"Probably," Laura said, shrugging.

They arrived at St. Agnes at noon. It looked exactly like when they left it.

"Not a thing has changed, has it?" Luca said, whistling.

"Nope," Laura said with a pouty face.

They went to the matron's office.

"Hello, Miss Maria," Laura said in a very low voice.

"Laura and Luca.... What are you two doing here?" The matron asked, looking startled.

"We just thought we'd come to see you," Luca said, resting his hand on Laura's shoulder.

"Why?"

"We know you have breast cancer," Laura said, clutching her necklace.

"How do you know that?" The matron asked, her eyes widened.

"Rudolfo told us," Luca said with a straight face.

"That guy Rudolfo could never keep his mouth shut, could he?" The matron said with a strained chuckle.

"How are you feeling?" Laura asked, concerned.

"Fine, dear. Laura, you're pregnant...?" The matron asked, eyeing Laura's big belly.

"Yes, I am, Miss Maria," Laura said, stroking her belly.

"Who's the father of the baby?" The matron asked, shifting her gaze from Laura to Luca.

"Luca, of course," Laura said, annoyed that the matron had even asked such a question.

"Are you two married?" The matron asked, folding her arms.

"Yes, we didn't have a baby out of wedlock," Luca said, sneering.

"Isn't it funny? I thought I was pregnant before I was diagnosed with breast cancer."

"Why do you say that?" Luca asked, raising his eyebrows.

"My breasts felt extremely tender and sore at the time, dear," the matron said, frowning.

"Laura's breasts are that way too now that she's pregnant," Luca said, caressing Laura's stomach.

"You're both good children. I should've treated you better," the matron said with a heavy sigh.

"It's okay, Miss Maria. No point in dwelling in the past," Luca said, looking away from her.

"I shouldn't have whipped you, Laura. It was uncalled for," the matron said remorsefully.

"I forgive you, Miss Maria," Laura said with a warm smile.

"I lied to you, Laura," the matron said, her head hanging in shame.

"About what?" Laura asked, looking her dead in the eye.

"Your sister didn't run away with the gardener," the matron said, unable to look her in the eye.

"I know," Laura said, gloomily.

"She was killed by Mr. Lorenzo," the matron said, catching a sob in her throat.

"I'm aware. Who do you think killed Mr. Lorenzo?" Luca asked, grimacing.

"I don't know..." The matron said, shaking her head.

"Me!" Luca cried.

"You killed Mr. Lorenzo?" The matron asked, looking alarmed.

"Yes, I went to prison for a year. How did you not hear about this?" Luca asked indignantly.

"I don't keep up with the news anymore, dear. I'm just awaiting my death," the matron said, feeling blue.

"Where is pastor James?" Laura asked, looking around the office.

"He's dead, dear," the matron said, her voice cracking.

"Pastor James is dead?" Luca asked, nearly shouting.

"Yes. He died from lung cancer," the matron said, tears pooling in her eyes.

"Really?" Laura asked in disbelief.

"Yes. He died two months after you both left," the matron said, sobbing.

"Is that why he looked so pale and sickly when we last saw him?" Luca asked, deep in thought.

"Yes."

"He's a monster," Luca said, balling his fists.

"I loved him," the matron said, holding her hands on her chest.

"He took Giulia's underwear," Laura said, glowering.

"I know that, dear," the matron said, nodding her head in agreement.

"What?" Laura asked, recoiling in disgust.

"I just didn't want to admit it. Pastor James told me all about it the day before he died."

"He waited till then to tell you about it?" Luca asked, fuming.

"He's a good man. You have to believe me," the matron said, joining her hands together.

"No, he's not," Laura said, scoffing.

"He suffered all his life. The man doesn't know what it's like to be at peace," the matron said, looking dejected.

"You think Luca and I haven't suffered?" Laura asked, moving closer to her.

"I'm not denying that," the matron said, backing away from her.

"You think Giulia hasn't suffered?" Laura asked, grinding her teeth.

"She definitely has, but-" the matron said, sweating profusely.

"I hope you rot in hell!" Laura screamed, shaking her by the shoulder.

"Please don't say that, Laura," the matron said, begging her.

"I hope both you and pastor James burn in flames," Laura said, boring her eyes into her.

"Laura!" The matron couldn't believe the words coming out of her mouth.

"You think you getting breast cancer and pastor James getting lung cancer was a mistake?"

"Please stop!" The matron said, covering her ears with both her hands.

"It is karma. God is punishing you for your sins," Laura said, raising her voice.

"You said you forgave me..." The matron's voice trailed off.

"I will forgive, but I will never forget," Laura said, glaring at her.

Laura and Luca stormed out of the children's home. They caught a bus to Modena. They reached their apartment at six in the evening.

"The gall of that woman!" Laura said, rolling her eyes.

"She is something else, I tell you," Luca said, resting his hands under his chin.

"Pastor James suffered all his life. Bullshit!" Laura said, incensed.

"Let's watch some TV and try to forget about that awful woman," Luca said, putting his arm around her shoulder.

"You're right," Laura said, taking deep breaths to calm herself down.

Rudolfo called us the next morning.

"Did you hear about Miss Maria?" Rudolfo asked, breathing heavily.

"What about her?" Luca asked, sounding troubled.

"She passed away last night. She supposedly died all alone in her dark and dingy room."

CHAPTER TWENTY-FIVE

ATONEMENT

"When I weep and fast, I must endure scorn;" (Psalm 69:10)

Laura was taking a nap on the couch in the living room when Luca was making breakfast.

"Laura, honey, come here and have some breakfast. I've made buttered toast and pomegranate juice," Luca called out to her from the kitchen.

"I don't want breakfast," Laura said, grumpily.

"Why not?" Luca asked with a confused countenance.

"I don't feel like it," Laura said, stifling a yawn.

"You can't afford to skip breakfast. It's the most important meal of the day. You need to eat at least for the baby's sake," Luca said in a firm tone.

"I can't eat anything today," Laura said, shaking her head.

"Why is that?" Luca asked with a blank look on his face.

"Today is the day Giulia went missing. It's been exactly five years since she went missing," Laura said in a somber tone.

"So?" Luca asked with a shrug.

"I'm commemorating her death. I won't eat anything," Laura said, fidgeting with her necklace.

"You can't do that," Luca said, lifting her chin tenderly.

"I can," Laura said, gazing into his eyes.

"You could've done that if you weren't pregnant. But you are, so you're not skipping breakfast. Not on my watch."

"I will skip, and there's nothing you can do about it," Laura said, thumbing her nose.

"That is our baby in there. You want our baby to starve?" Luca asked, pointing at her belly.

"No...."

"The doctor said you can't skip any meals. Not when you're pregnant," Luca said, placing a hand on her tummy.

"I'm sick of you telling me what to do. You're not my father," Laura said, grouchily.

"I'm the baby's father, and as the baby's father, I'm telling you to eat your breakfast," Luca said, losing his cool.

"I'm not eating breakfast, and that's final," Laura said, huffing.

"You're eating and that's final. If it means I've to force-feed you, then so be it," Luca said in a stern tone.

"Luca, no-"

Laura leapt up and waddled towards the kitchen.

"Where are you going, Laura?" Luca said, chuckling.

"Don't come close to me," Laura said, looking back to make sure he wasn't following her.

Luca quickly sneaked up behind her and carried her in his arms.

"Where do you think you're going?" Luca asked, grinning at her.

"Put me down!" Laura said, banging her fists against his chest.

Luca pinned her down to the couch. She tried to get up this time, but she couldn't. Luca brought a plate of buttered toast and a glass of pomegranate juice to where she was lying.

"I didn't spend all morning making breakfast just so you can waste it," Luca said, sitting beside her on the couch.

He forcefully opened her mouth and shoved a piece of toast into her mouth.

"Luca, stop! Mmmm," Laura said as crumbs of the toast flew out of her mouth.

"It's delicious, isn't it?" Luca said with a sparkle in his eyes.

He pinched her nostrils, opened her mouth again and made her drink the pomegranate juice in one sip.

"Atta girl," Luca said, ruffling her hair.

Laura stared daggers at Luca.

"I told you I wasn't going to eat anything, and you force-fed me. How dare you!" Laura said, scowling at him.

"You don't have a choice in the matter. I'm sorry. The baby you're carrying is mine too," Luca said, pouting his lips.

"You don't understand how much this fast means to me," Laura said, hurting.

"Laura, you're six months pregnant. Every meal matters. You've to eat for the baby's sake," Luca said with pleading eyes.

"My baby will be fine if it doesn't eat for one day," Laura said, folding her arms across her chest.

"No, it won't," Luca said, stroking her hair. "Laura, you're being stubborn."

"I'm being stubborn?" Laura asked, scoffing.

"Yes."

"If you're not stubborn, then why did you force-feed me?" Laura asked, stomping her feet.

"Because I had no other choice," Luca said, raising his voice.

"You're not sleeping with me tonight," Laura said, moving away from him.

"What? Where will I sleep then?" Luca asked, scratching his head.

"You're sleeping on this couch," Laura said, drumming her fingers on the couch.

"This is ridiculous!" Luca exclaimed, throwing his hands up in the air.

"Never mess with a pregnant woman," Laura said, wagging a finger in front of Luca's face.

"I've learned my lesson," Luca said, smirking.

CHAPTER TWENTY-SIX

RECOLLECTION

"The more you worry, the more likely you are to have bad dreams..." (Ecclesiastes 5:3)

The day I was killed was particularly a pleasant one. Laura woke me up that morning.

"Get up, sleepyhead," Laura said, pulling the blanket off me.

"I don't want to...." I said, groaning.

"We have to eat our breakfast," Laura said, shaking me by the shoulder.

"What are we having for breakfast? If it's something I don't like, I'm not coming for breakfast."

"I heard we're having biscotti and latte," Laura said, stroking her chin.

"Really?" I asked, jolting awake.

"Yes! Are you coming now?" Laura asked impatiently.

"Yeah!"

We rushed towards the dining room, hand in hand.

"Come on, Giulia. I saved you a seat," Luca said, beckoning me to sit with him.

I sat next to Luca and Laura sat opposite him.

Luca's left hand lingered on my inner thigh. He was madly in love with me.

"I saved you some of this biscotti, or else Rudolfo would've eaten the whole thing," Luca said, looking at Rudolfo disapprovingly.

"Aww, thanks!" I said, smitten with him.

When Laura saw Luca's elbow brushing against my breasts, she turned green with envy.

"You two lovebirds are making me sick!" Laura asked, gagging.

"Yeah, like get a room," Rudolfo said as he shoved a piece of biscotti into his mouth.

"Are you jealous of me, Laura?" I asked, sneering.

"No, why would I be jealous of you?" Laura asked, scoffing.

"Because you like Luca," I said, looking her straight in the eye.

"I don't like Luca. Who said I like him? I hate him!" Laura said, grinding her teeth.

"No, you don't. Stop lying," I said, clicking my tongue.

"I'm not lying, Giulia," Laura said, banging her fists on the table.

"Anyhoo, you can't fall in love with Luca. You hear me? He is mine," I said, kissing his right cheek.

"Oh yeah?" Laura asked, crossly.

"Yeah, I'm gonna marry him one day, and have his babies," I said, smirking.

"Who cares?" Laura said, rolling her eyes.

"You care," I said, tittering.

"I'm gonna marry someone who is way more handsome than Luca anyway," Laura said, smugly.

"I doubt it," I said, snickering.

"You think I won't. You just wait and watch," Laura said, clenching her fists.

"I doubt there's any guy in Maranello who is more handsome than Luca," I said, winking at Luca.

"I need to leave. Excuse me," Laura said, getting up from her seat.

Laura ran to her bedroom. Luca followed her to the bedroom.

"Hey, what's wrong?" Luca asked, closing the bedroom door gently.

"I hate Giulia!" Laura said, fuming.

"You know she's only joking, right?" Luca said, sitting next to her in bed.

"Why would she joke about that?" Laura asked, pouting.

"Don't take it to heart," Luca said, gazing into her eyes.

"Easy for you to say. You're not the one she's teasing," Laura said, hurting.

"She's not teasing you," Luca said, raising his voice.

"Yes, she is. She is saying I'm ugly," Laura said, blubbering.

"She never said you're ugly," Luca said, wiping the tears from her eyes.

"She's saying I won't marry a handsome guy like you because I'm ugly," Laura said, sniffling.

"You think I'm handsome?" Luca asked as his eyes lit up.

"No!"

"You just said so..." Luca said, looking confused.

"You're handsome, but you're not that handsome," Laura said, folding her arms.

"You're such a liar," Luca said, booping her nose.

Luca convinced her to come back to the dining room.

"I'm not talking to you, Giulia," Laura said, taking a big bite of the biscotti.

"Fine with me," I said, munching on the biscotti.

"Luca thinks I'm prettier than you," Laura said, beaming.

"I never said that," Luca said, glaring at her.

"You mark my words, he's gonna marry me one day," Laura said, taking his hands in hers.

"We'll see about that," I said in a mocking tone.

Lord knows that turned out to be true.

"You wanna play with us in the garden," Laura asked, barging into my bedroom later that day.

"No."

"Mr. Lorenzo is coming here tonight," Laura said, shifting her weight from one foot to the other.

"Oh, really?" I asked, raising my eyebrows.

"Yeah," Laura said, smiling at me.

"You go ahead. I don't feel like playing," I said, looking away from her.

"Okay," Laura said, distractedly.

Laura skipped along to the garden. I went to the chapel instead.

While I was praying, I had a vision.

In my vision, I was being strangled by a man. I pleaded with him to stop, but he didn't.

I was horrified. I fled to the children's room, sobbing. I ran straight to my bedroom without a word. Laura spotted me from the garden.

"Hey, what's wrong?" Laura asked, quietly entering my bedroom.

"Nothing," I said, fighting back my tears.

"I know when something's wrong with you. We're twins, remember?" Laura said, plopping down on the bed.

"I had a vision..." I said, cradling myself back and forth in bed.

"Okay, so?"

"I was getting strangled to death in my vision," I said, my voice cracking.

"What? Really?" Laura asked, looking horrified.

"He didn't stop, Laura," I said, covering my face with my hands.

"Who is this man?" Laura asked, narrowing her eyes.

"I don't know. His face was blurry," I said, frowning.

"Well, that's not very helpful, is it?" Laura asked, looking disappointed.

"It seemed too real to ignore," I said, shuddering.

"I'm sure it's not real. It's your silly little head playing tricks with you," Laura asked, knocking me on the head.

"I guess...." I said with a shrug.

"You've been feeling down lately. You need to get out more often," Laura said, resting a hand on my shoulder.

"You're right," I said, shaking my head.

"Just take a shower and get some rest. You'll be alright when you wake up," Laura asked, squeezing my shoulder.

I took a shower and went to bed as Laura told me to.

Then, I had that nasty vision again. This time the man was in my bedroom. He pounced at me and smothered me with a pillow to drown out my cries.

"Help me! Help me!" I screamed at the top of my lungs.

Luca came dashing into my bedroom.

"What's wrong, Giulia?" Luca asked, looking alarmed.

"I saw that man again," I said, pointing at the man standing in front of me.

"Which man?" Luca asked, looking around the bedroom.

"The man who is trying to kill me. I can't see his face. It's blurred."

"You're just having a nightmare," Luca said, sitting beside me in bed.

"No. It's real, Luca. It's going to happen. I'm going to get killed," I said as my eyes swelled with tears.

"Nonsense! You're not getting killed, Giulia," Luca said, stroking my hair.

"I'm scared, Luca...." I said, whimpering like a child.

"You want me to sleep here with you," Luca asked, rubbing my back.

"Yes..." I said with a slight nod.

Luca kissed my forehead and he wrapped his arms around my waist.

"I feel safe with you beside me, Luca," I said, taking a deep breath.

"I feel safe beside you too, Giulia," Luca said, breathing into my neck.

We slept till noon in each other's arms. I didn't have that awful vision after that.

At noon, Laura came to my bedroom to call me for lunch. She saw me lying next to Luca and lost it.

"Giulia, come for lunch," Laura said, leaning against the bedroom door.

"What?" I asked, getting up.

"Don't you want to have lunch?" Laura asked with a sullen expression.

"Yes.""Come on then. Call Luca," Laura said, eyeing Luca out of the corner of her eye.

Laura banged the bedroom door shut after her.

"Luca..." I whispered.

"Uhhh, what is it?" Luca asked, rubbing his eyes.

"Luca, we need to have our lunch," I said, gently poking his cheeks.

"Oh, yeah...." Luca said, stretching his arms.

"Come on. Wake up," I said, tapping him on the shoulder.

We went to the dining room to have our lunch, but Laura was nowhere to be seen.

"Where is Laura?" I asked, sitting next to Luca.

"She is having food poisoning, so she won't be joining us for lunch today," Rudolfo said, eyeing the plate of mushroom risotto set aside for Laura.

Laura wasn't poisoned with food. She was poisoned with envy. She threw up everything she had for breakfast into the toilet bowl.

CHAPTER TWENTY-SEVEN

BETRAYAL

"And while they were eating, he said, "Truly I tell you, one of you will betray me." (Matthew 26:21)

The reason Laura and I slept in separate rooms was that Laura got her periods and I didn't. We were sleeping together till then. The matron said she was impure and that I was still pure, and that I shouldn't lie next to someone who is impure.

When Laura started getting her periods, her breasts got bigger. I was jealous of her. I was worried Luca would start falling for her because of her big boobs. My flat chest would be no match for her big boobs. But Luca still chose me over her. He liked my boobs better than hers.

Laura thought that when she got big boobs, Luca would start hitting on her, but he didn't. Every other boy at St. Agnes ogled at her boobs, but not Luca. He is a gentleman like that.

I knew that Laura didn't have food poisoning. She was always such a liar. She was mad that Luca was sleeping with me, and not with her. She saw us lying in bed as husband and wife, and she couldn't stand it. She felt sick to her stomach. She wanted to lie next to him as his wife.

I had my lunch and went back to bed. Luca didn't join me this time. Laura was busy throwing up in her room.

I was getting worried for Laura. It felt like I was getting under her skin on purpose. I told myself I wouldn't do that from that day onwards.

The truth is I wanted Laura to marry a more handsome guy than Luca. I wanted only what was best for her. I was only pulling her leg. I didn't really mean anything I said.

It's true that I'm jealous of Laura carrying Luca's baby, but I'm also happy for her. If any woman is going to have Luca's child. It has to be Laura.

I'm actually pleased Laura is naming the baby after me. It means she still cares about me. Despite being six months pregnant, she was going to fast for me. I didn't want her to fast though. It is not good for her or the baby. I'm glad Luca force-fed her. Laura can be really stupid sometimes.

Laura has been thinking of me throughout her pregnancy. She still believes I'm somewhere out there waiting for her. She often cries in her sleep. It might be the pregnancy hormones. Who knows?

I take back everything I said before. I don't want Laura to have a miscarriage. I want her to carry the baby to full term.

I want her to experience the joy of motherhood. I want Luca to stand by her side while she gives birth to the baby. I want him to hold the baby in his arms before giving it to her.

I want her to see her child grow up to become a smart and beautiful young woman.

I want Laura to have more babies with Luca. They will be one big happy family. That's what I REALLY want for her.

I love her to death. There's nobody in this world who loves her more than me. Not even her sweet and loving husband, Luca.

I loved her when she was in my mother's womb with me and I'll continue to love her for infinity.

On the night I was killed, Mr. Lorenzo came to the children's home. It was raining cats and dogs.

"Miss Maria, I want you to bring me one of these children. A girl child please," Mr. Lorenzo said, drenched in rainwater.

"Which one?" The matron asked, blinking her eyes.

"Probably one who hasn't had her periods yet," Mr. Lorenzo said to her in a very low voice.

"Why does that matter?" The matron asked, scratching her head.

"I don't know, because girls who have their periods are impure," Mr. Lorenzo said, shuddering.

"Okay, I know a pretty girl who hasn't had her periods yet. Her twin sister has had periods though."

"A twin, you say," Mr. Lorenzo asked with a creepy smile.

"Yes."

"Interesting. Bring her to me," Mr. Lorenzo said, stroking his chin.

It's not that he didn't want girls with periods because they were impure. He didn't want them because he was afraid they'd get pregnant if he raped them, and he'd get busted.

I was sleeping in my bed when the matron gently knocked on my door.

"Giulia, open the door."

I staggered towards the bedroom door and opened it.

"What is it, Miss Maria?" I asked, rubbing my eyes.

"Mr. Lorenzo wants to talk to you," the matron said, smiling at me.

"But it's three at midnight," I said, droopily.

"I know, but Mr. Lorenzo wants to speak only with you," the matron said, resting a hand on my shoulder.

"Why? Am I in trouble?" I asked, crossly.

"What? No! He's been closely watching all you children for a while now. He thinks you're the best child at St. Agnes. So, he wants to reward you. That's all."

"Really?" I asked with a twinkle in my eye.

"Yes."

"Are you telling me the truth?" I asked, eyeing her suspiciously.

"Yes, why would I lie about this? You can always trust Miss Maria," the matron said with an insincere smile.

"What will he give me?" I asked, really hoping it wouldn't be a pocket bible or a rosary.

"He told me he'll read you a bedtime story and then give you some candies," the matron said, unable to look me in the eye.

"Candies?" I asked, my eyes widened.

"Yes."

"Can I bring Laura along? She loves candies!" I said with a bright smile.

"No! Laura is not the one the owner wants to talk to. It is you!" the matron said, scowling at me.

"Okay," I said, feeling a bit shocked.

"These candies are only for you. Don't give it to her. You hear me?" The matron asked, shaking me by the shoulder.

"Yes, Miss Maria," I said, feeling dizzy.

She led me to the room where Mr. Lorenzo was waiting for me.

"Hello, little girl," Mr. Lorenzo greeted me.

"Hello, Mr. Lorenzo," I said with my hands behind my back.

"What is your name, dear?" Mr. Lorenzo asked, gazing into my aqua eyes.

"Giulia," I said, beaming at him.

"That's a beautiful name, dear," Mr. Lorenzo said, tousling my hair.

"Thanks," I said with a coy smile.

He never remembered my name though he thought it was beautiful.

"You know why I called you here, dear?" Mr. Lorenzo asked, sitting cross-legged on a chair.

"Yes," I said, nodding my head.

"You're the purest girl here at St. Agnes, and it must be rewarded," Mr. Lorenzo said, lifting

my chin and closely examining my face.

"Are you going to give me candies?" I asked, looking at him expectantly.

"No," Mr. Lorenzo said with a chuckle.

"Miss Maria told me you'll read me a bedtime story and then give me candies."

"She was lying, dear," Mr. Lorenzo said, sighing.

"Really?" I asked, feeling down in the dumps.

"Yes," Mr. Lorenzo said, gawking at my body.

"So, you don't have candies then?" I asked, pouting my lips.

"What we're going to have is something that's so much better than candies," Mr. Lorenzo said, leering at me.

"What is it?" I asked, wondering what could be better than candies.

"Do you know what sex is?" Mr. Lorenzo asked, moving closer to me.

"No," I said, shaking my head in pure confusion.

"That's what we're going to have tonight," Mr. Lorenzo said, taking my hands in his.

"Is it a candy?" I asked with eager eyes.

"No, no, child. God, I love children!" Mr. Lorenzo said, guffawing.

CHAPTER TWENTY-EIGHT

MURDER

"You shall not murder." (Exodus 20:13)

Mr. Lorenzo asked the matron to close the door and leave me alone with him. She obeyed him and did as he told her.

"We're going to have ourselves a little fun," Mr. Lorenzo said, rubbing his hands together.

He unbuckled his pants, removed his boxers and dropped them to the floor.

"You wanna touch this?" Mr. Lorenzo asked, holding out his shaft for me to touch.

I hesitantly went over to him and touched his penis and it became hard.

"You like it?" He asked, grinning at me.

I shook my head and he roared with laughter.

"How is this better than caramelle?" I asked, frowning.

"Oh, it is. Trust me. Remove your panties, dear," Mr. Lorenzo said in a sugary voice.

I followed his instructions and pulled down my panties.

"You're a virgin, right?" Mr. Lorenzo asked, gawking at my nether region.

"What is that?" I asked, looking confused.

"Have you slept with a guy before?" Mr. Lorenzo asked, really hoping I didn't.

"Yes."

"But did you have sex? Did he put this down there?" Mr. Lorenzo asked, clutching his erect penis.

"No."

"Yeah, that's what I thought. That's good," Mr. Lorenzo said, sounding pleased.

"Okay..."

He came closer to me and I moved further away from him.

"Lie on that bed, dear," Mr. Lorenzo said, pointing at the dusty cot in the corner of the room.

I went over to the bed and lay in it. The only source of light in that room was an oil lamp on the bedside table.

He got on top of me and hiked up my frock.

"We can get this over with soon. You just lie still like a good girl," Mr. Lorenzo said and kissed the nape of my neck while spreading my legs wide open.

He forcefully thrust his big penis into my tiny vagina and started rocking back and forth hurriedly.

"This really hurts, Mr. Lorenzo," I said, wincing.

"Hush, pretty girl," Mr. Lorenzo said, shushing me.

"Please stop, Mr. Lorenzo," I said, my lips quivering.

I flailed my arms and legs.

"Quit squirming," Mr. Lorenzo said in a vexed voice.

He pinned my arms to the bed and pressed his knees against my legs.

"Let go of me!" I yelled, lying spread-eagled.

"Stop it, I say," Mr. Lorenzo said, clicking his tongue.

"Miss Maria, he's hurting me!" I screamed aloud.

He wrapped his hands around my neck.

"Stop screaming," Mr. Lorenzo said, grimacing.

"Miss Maria, help me!" I yelled, trying to wrench his hands off of my neck.

He started strangling me.

"Mr. Lorenzo, please stop. I beg of you," I said with pleading eyes.

He continued to choke me till I was out of breath.

"I can't breathe! I can't breathe!" I cried, my voice cracking and my face turning blue.

"Shut up, little girl!" Mr. Lorenzo shouted, gritting his teeth and throttling me harshly.

He tightened his grip around my neck till I went limp.

"Little girl, are you alright?" Mr. Lorenzo asked, waving his hands in my face.

I was no longer breathing. He felt my pulse. There were no signs of life.

"Oh, God! Let her not be dead," Mr. Lorenzo said, catching a sob in his throat.

He violently shook me and slapped me across the face, but in vain.

"Miss Maria, come here," Mr. Lorenzo shouted from the bedroom.

The matron came rushing into the room.

"Can you check her pulse?" Mr. Lorenzo said, getting away from my body.

She checked my pulse and looked at the owner with dread.

"Why are you not wearing your pants? Why are her panties around her ankles? What in God's name did you do to this girl?"

"I think I may have killed her......" Mr. Lorenzo said, horror-struck.

"Is that blood I see?" The matron asked, pointing at the blood-soaked bedsheet. "Did you rape her, Mr. Lorenzo?"

The matron put her hand under my frock. She felt something sticky on her hand.

"Oh, God! That's blood!" The matron shrieked in horror.

"What will I do? I didn't mean to kill her..." Mr. Lorenzo said, looking downcast.

"How could I have been such an idiot? I should've known why you were specifically asking for a girl who hasn't had her periods yet. You were afraid you'd get the girl pregnant, weren't you?" The matron asked, snarling.

"Please forgive me, Miss Maria," Mr. Lorenzo said, begging her.

"There's only one thing to do," the matron said, heaving a sigh.

The matron went to the storage room and brought back a huge sack.

"We'll have to dispose of her body," the matron said, looking the owner dead in the eye.

"Oh, God!" Mr. Lorenzo gasped loudly.

The matron removed my white frock and my panties and neatly put them in a Ziploc bag. She left the necklace on my neck though. She shoved my naked corpse into the sack.

"I'll dump this sack in the huge junkyard behind St. Agnes," the matron said, grunting.

"Okay, good idea," Mr. Lorenzo said, sounding relieved.

When she was dragging the sack out of the room and down the corridor, Laura spotted her.

"What are you carrying there, Miss Maria?" Laura asked, pointing at the sack.

"Just a sack of grains," the matron said, smiling at her.

"Oh, okay," Laura said, smiling back at her.

"Why haven't you slept yet?" The matron asked, narrowing her eyes.

"I just want to grab a glass of water. I'm thirsty," Laura said, gulping.

"Drink from the faucet in your washroom. Go to your bedroom at once," the matron said in a stern tone.

"Okay, Miss Maria," Laura said, grumpily.

Laura quietly went back to her bedroom and closed the bedroom door.

The matron dragged the sack all the way to the junkyard and tossed it atop a mountain of garbage.

She dusted off her hands after she was done with the dirty work.

"Rest in peace, Giulia," the matron whispered and walked away with a heavy heart.

CHAPTER TWENTY-NINE

FORGIVENESS

'Then Peter came to Jesus and asked, "Lord, how many times shall I forgive my brother or sister who sins against me? Up to seven times?"

Jesus answered, "I tell you, not seven times, but seventy-seven times.' (Matthew 18:21-22)

When I was only four years old, my mom told me and my sister to love those who sin against us. I thought it was absurd at the time. How can you love someone whom you hate? It's impossible!

"There will come a time when someone will sin against you," my mother warned us. "You should forgive them not once, not twice, but seventy times seven."

How can you forgive someone seventy-seven times? Shouldn't once suffice? Besides, seventy-seven was an oddly specific number.

It was much later I found out that she was quoting from one of the verses in the Bible.

My mother forgave my father even though he abused her. He hated that she didn't bear him any sons. He despised my mother and us.

I wish God had taken away my father alone and not my mother. If my mother were alive, I wouldn't have died.

Even if I was raped and killed, my mom would've slit the throat of Mr. Lorenzo herself.

But Luca took her place. He killed Mr. Lorenzo for me and served his sentence.

If my mom were alive, she would've loved Luca very much. She would've seen him as the son she never had. Luca came into Laura's and my life right after our mother died.

He was one of the boys I first spoke to at St. Agnes.

Luca and Laura will never find it in their hearts to forgive Mr. Lorenzo, nor will I.

He robbed me of my life. If it weren't for him, Luca and I would be together now, and Laura would be with a guy more handsome than Luca.

I trusted Mr. Lorenzo. I thought he was a good man.

Because of him, we had all those fancy meals back at the children's home.

The worst thing is, he has a wife and a girl child. Now that kid is fatherless. It's better to be fatherless than have a father who is a pedophile and a rapist.

He preyed on the orphans because he knew there would be no one who would fight for them.

How could he peacefully lie in bed knowing he'd raped and murdered a young girl?

I can't forgive Mr. Lorenzo even if that's probably what my mother would want me to do.

Perhaps I can forgive the pastor for taking my underwear. Perhaps I can forgive the matron for all the wrongs she did to me.

Maybe I'm lying to myself. Maybe I can't forgive the matron after all.

When it comes to all the sins the matron had committed, there is a whole list for that:

The List of Wrongs of Miss Maria

1. She was a hypocrite. She always talked about chastity, but wasn't chaste herself.

2. She was a big-time liar. She lied about me running away with the gardener.

3. She valued the life of humans over animals. She didn't think animals were worth living.

4. She was an abuser. She whipped Laura to death.

5. She had an immoral relationship. She had sex with the pastor despite knowing it was off-limits.

6. She was a snitch. She threatened to expose the cook's secret of having a child out of wedlock to the owner of the children's home.

7. She wanted the kids at St. Agnes to starve. If it were entirely up to her, she'd serve the children nothing but stale gruel and apples.

8. She didn't like seeing boys and girls talking to each other or holding hands.

9. She told Luca that Laura was a bad influence on him. That is so not true. Laura was and will continue to be a good influence on him. She always brings out the best in him.

10. She was a traitor. She told me I could trust her and took me to Mr. Lorenzo like how a lamb is taken to the butcher to be slaughtered.

11. She was an accomplice to my murder. She shoved my body into a sack and dumped it in the junkyard behind the children's home.

12. She knew the pastor took my underwear and kept quiet about it.

13. She tried to justify the pastor's actions till the very end. She said he had suffered all his life and didn't know what it was like to be at peace.

14. She never reported my murder to the police. She never testified against Mr. Lorenzo in court.

15. She tried to take away my sister's necklace. The only thing she has to remember me by.

16. She hated Laura because she was close to Luca and because she was my twin sister.

Despite all this, my mom would want me to forgive her. How can I? This is why I don't like the idea of forgiveness. People can do horrible things and get away with them if they're forgiven.

I'm not ready to forgive the matron just yet.

I will forgive her one day, but that day will not be anytime soon.

My mom and I are not that different. She was also raped. After my mom had me and my sister, my dad demanded they try to make a baby again. When my mother refused, my father had his way with her. My mother got pregnant again, but she suffered a miscarriage three months later.

That's when my father started really hating her. He thought she had a miscarriage on purpose to spite him.

When mom found out she was pregnant with her third child, she spent sleepless days and nights at Church praying to God to bless her with a son.

But God didn't give her a son.

It's not that He didn't listen to my mother's countless prayers for a son, it's that He didn't want my father to have the satisfaction of having a son after abusing my mother.

It seems my mother had forgiven my father, but not God.

I will never forgive my father for what he did to my mother. He had no right to abuse my mother just because she couldn't give him a boy child.

My father is one of those nincompoops who think that the woman is solely responsible for determining the gender of the child.

He doesn't realize it's the father's sperm that determines the baby's gender. The mother's egg will bear the X chromosome. If the father's sperm bears the X chromosome, it will be a girl baby. If the father's sperm bears the Y chromosome, it will be a boy child.

How is it my mother's fault that my father's sperm always bears the X chromosome?

When the doctor said it was his sperm that determined the baby's gender, he didn't like it one bit.

He beat my mom once they came back home. He told my mom the doctor was siding with her because she was a woman and because women are weak and can't speak for themselves. He was a sexist porco!

I will never understand why my mother married a misogynist. My mother was probably forced to marry him because of her parents. My dad's side of the family was filthy rich after all.

Luca is the antithesis of my father, and that's why I fell in love with him.

They are like chalk and cheese. Like night and day.

He loves girl children. He is such a gentleman!

If Luca met my father, he would've hated him to death. They would've never gotten along.

How could my mom forgive a monster like my dad?

If my mother were still alive, would she have forgiven Mr. Lorenzo for what he did to me? I don't think so.

I hope my father, the matron, the pastor and Mr. Lorenzo all burn in hell for eternity. Screw forgiveness!

CHAPTER THIRTY

CLOSURE

"Those who walk uprightly enter into peace; they find rest as they lie in death." (Isaiah 57:2)

After the matron died, the children's home was shut down. All the children at St. Agnes were relocated to other children's homes in nearby towns. It's probably for the best.

My bones were uncovered in the sack while the mountain of garbage was being cleared out. The children's home is being torn down because a children's hospital is going to be built in its place.

When my bones were identified as mine, I was given a proper burial. Laura and Luca were the only ones who attended my funeral. The sky was overcast and it later rained heavily that day.

My sister is heavily pregnant now. She can barely stand straight.

Laura and Luca often visited my grave. They wanted to keep me company at all times.

Laura and Luca visited my tomba again today. They brought me a bouquet of white roses.

Laura bent over to place the bouquet on my grave and winced in pain.

"Hello, Giulia. How are you today? We just came here to check on you. We hope you're keeping well," Laura said, exhaling softly.

"Laura insisted that we come to see you today. I skipped work today to come here," Luca said, looking upset.

"I brought you these rose bianche. I know just how much you love rose bianche," Laura said with a sad smile.

"Laura spent almost an hour picking out these flowers from the flower shop. They're very fresh," Luca said with gleaming eyes.

"I'm eight months pregnant now. I have a hard time walking," Laura said, swaying from side to side.

"Trust me, she does. I have to carry her around the house," Luca said, grinning at her.

"I'm naming the baby after you, Giulia. She will be Giulia Jr. Don't you like it?" Laura asked, stroking her belly.

"She didn't tell me she was naming the baby after you," Luca said, sulking.

"This baby will grow up to become smart and beautiful just like you," Laura said, looking down at her big belly.

"Ain't that the truth?" Luca said with a sparkle in his eyes.

"Did you hear they're building a children's hospital in place of the children's home?" Laura asked, sounding pleased.

"Isn't that just wonderful?" Luca said, unable to contain his joy.

"The pastor died of lung cancer and the matron died of breast cancer. You had something to do with that, didn't you?"

"Giulia would never do something like that," Luca said, shaking his head.

"Then you don't know my sister well enough," Laura said, huffing.

"I guess not," Luca said with a shrug.

"You're also the one who burnt down the house of the three men who harassed me, aren't you? Luca says it's divine justice, but I think it's your justice. Giulia's justice," Laura said, smirking.

"No, it isn't," Luca said, rolling his eyes.

"Yes, it is," Laura said, stomping her feet. "Our mother told us to forgive those who sin against us seventy times seven, but our mother didn't know any better."

"Your mother had a heart of gold," Luca said, resting a hand on Laura's shoulder.

"She did, but she was also a fool," Laura said, biting her bottom lip.

"Why is that?" Luca asked, looking muddled.

"She should've never forgiven my father," Laura said, looking away from him.

"Why not?"

"He abused her for goodness' sake," Laura said, her voice squeaking.

"I know that."

"There's something I've never told you about my mom," Laura said, twiddling her thumbs.

"What is that?" Luca asked, gazing into her eyes.

"My mom was also raped by my dad," Laura said in a very low voice.

"What, really?" Luca asked, looking horrified.

"Yes. When she refused to have a baby for the third time, he took her by force," Laura said, fuming.

"That's horrible!" Luca exclaimed, gasping loudly.

"Still my mother forgave him," Laura said, holding her hands on her chest.

"Did she get pregnant?" Luca asked, raising his eyebrows.

"Yes, but she suffered a miscarriage three months later," Laura said, fighting back her tears.

"Twins themselves are a handful. Why did your dad want a third child? " Luca asked, narrowing his eyes.

"He wanted a boy child," Laura said, tears welling up in her eyes.

"Was he for real?" Luca asked, gritting his teeth.

"He was mad that his two children were both girls," Laura said as tears spilled down her cheeks.

I could feel her pain like it was my own.

"Unbelievable," Luca said, resting his hands under his chin.

"My dad thought women were weak and useless," Laura said, clutching her chest.

"What a bigot!"

"I'll never forgive him," Laura said, balling her fists.

"You shouldn't have to," Luca said, squeezing her shoulder.

"It was my mom, my sister, and me against him," Laura said, pouting.

"I can only imagine," Luca said, gloomily.

"It pains me to think I'm his daughter," Laura said, hurting.

"You're nothing like him. You hear me?" Luca said, holding her face in his hands.

"Yes."

"Your dad was a monster. But you, you're an angel," Luca said, looking at her with tender affection.

"Oh, you're a flatterer, aren't you?" Laura said, her face turning beet-red.

"I'm being serious, Laura," Luca said in a serious tone.

"Okay."

"Even this daughter of ours will be nothing like him," Luca said, rubbing her belly in circles.

"If he were alive, he would take back everything he ever said about girls after he sees my Giulia," Laura said with a proud smile.

"Something tells me he would've been good friends with Mr. Lorenzo, the pastor and the matron."

"No doubt about that," Laura said with a straight face.

"They're probably friends with the devil," Luca said with a scornful glance.

"Yeah, or his minions," Laura said, sneering.

"They're probably wiping his ass or fanning him with flames in hell as we speak," Luca said, smirking.

"Maybe," Laura said, chuckling.

I was giggling listening to them cracking jokes about the three of them. They always knew how to cheer me up.

"Will you go back to work after you have the baby?" Luca asked, concerned.

"Definitely. We need money for the baby," Laura said, placing a hand on her belly.

"You don't have to work if you don't want to," Luca said, resting a hand on Laura's shoulder.

"I want to. Where else would I work?" Laura asked with a glum expression.

"You can always work with me at the grocery store," Luca said, smiling at her.

"Really?" Laura asked, her eyes widened.

"Yes. There's an opening for the post of a cashier. Adriana is quitting her job," Luca said, stretching his arms.

"Why?"

"She's moving to Milan with her boyfriend and her baby. She told me he got a job transfer."

"I'll work with you," Laura said, clapping her hands together.

"Oh, my God. Yes!" Luca said as he did his little happy dance.

"I hated my job anyway. Don't want more men hitting on me," Laura said, flinching.

"No, we don't want that," Luca said, shaking his head.

"You and I can work together at the store. Our daughter can come to the store after school."

"Yes! Then we can all go out for ice-creams," Luca said, dreamy-eyed.

"Or maybe a movie," Laura said, tapping her middle finger on her chin. "Or maybe both."

"If she has a sister, what would you name her?" Luca asked, stroking his chin.

"I don't know. I'll probably name her after my mother, Amelia," Laura said with a bright smile.

"Amelia. That's a beautiful name!" Luca said, beaming at her.

"I know right!" Laura said with a twinkle in her eye.

"If we had a boy child?" Luca asked, scratching the back of his neck.

"Luca..."

"My name?" Luca asked, pointing at himself.

"Luca Jr.," Laura said with a big grin on her face.

"Nice! Or we can name him Aurelio," Luca said, staring into space.

"Aurelio?"

"Yes, that's my dad's name," Luca said with a warm smile.

"Aurelio or Amelia.... I like that," Laura said, bobbing her head.

Just then, it started drizzling. Laura and Luca's rental car was parked outside the cemetery.

"It's time to go," Luca said, holding out the palm of his hand to touch the raindrops.

"Yes," Laura said, covering her head with her hands.

Luca led her to a rusty red car. Laura got in the passenger seat, and Luca got in the driver's seat and closed the car doors.

"Ready to go?" Luca asked, starting the car.

"Yes," Laura said, looking distracted.

Laura looked at my grave and there I was, holding the bouquet of white roses close to my chest.

"Laura, what do you want for breakfast?" Luca asked, facing her.

Laura didn't respond. She just stared at me.

"Hello? Earth to Laura!" Luca said, waving his hands in front of her face.

I looked back at her and smiled. I mouthed the words "thank you" and placed the bouquet back on my grave.

"Laura, dear, what do you want to eat for breakfast?"

I walked away from my grave, dead leaves crunching beneath my feet and soon disappeared into thin air.

Laura never saw me after that. My soul was finally at peace.

Epilogue

A few hours after returning from the cemetery, Laura was lying in bed when her hand brushed against something soft and furry.

"Oh, what is that?" Laura exclaimed, gripping her big belly and slowly sitting up in bed.

Her jaw dropped and her eyes nearly popped out of her sockets when she saw what was in front of her.

Her charming husband, Luca, was holding a snow-white kitten in his hands. It could not be more than a week old.

"Where did you find her?" Laura asked, unable to conceal her excitement.

"Him. It's a male kitten. I found this little guy in the bushes in front of our house," Luca said, beaming like a child.

"I love him! Can we keep him? Please! Can we keep him, please?" Laura asked with pleading eyes.

"Yes, of course. That's why I brought him to you," Luca said, planting a gentle kiss on the tip of the kitten's nose.

"What will we name him?" Laura asked, unable to take her eyes away from the fluffball.

"Rudolfo," Luca said jokingly.

"Why not?" Laura said chuckling.

"I was just joking, Laura...." Luca said, his face turning serious.

"No, no. I know that. It's a good name for this kitty though," Laura said, booping its tiny nose.

The kitten suddenly meowed and leapt out of Luca's hands. It brushed its head against Laura's stomach and purred softly.

"He loves baby Giulia," Laura murmured, catching a sob in her throat.

"Rudolfo sure does," Luca said, getting emotional as well. Tears soon started rolling down his smooth cheeks. He didn't love anyone in the world more than his beloved Laura and his dear Giulia.

The kitten took a long stretch, curled into a ball and rested on Laura's lap. Luca kissed his beautiful wife's forehead and got into bed with her. The sunlight filtered through the curtains and cast a warm glow on all their faces.

The End

Glossary List

1. È la vita - It is life

2. È vero - That is true

3. Puttana - Whore or Prostitute

4. Cagna - Bitch

5. Pedofilo - Pedophile

6. Mutandine - Underwear or Panties

7. Pene - Penis

8. Cazzo - Dick or Male genitalia

9. Tette - Breasts

10. Moffetta - Skunk

11. Capezzolo - Nipples

12. La piovre - A famous Italian Television Series

13. Lucky Luke - a 1984 animated television series based on the comic book series of the same name created by the Belgian cartoonist and creator of the franchise Morris.

14. Anima - Soul

15. Frittata - An egg-based Italian dish, similar to an omelette.

16. Biscotti - Italian almond biscuits originating in the city of Prato, Tuscany.

17. Caramelle - Candies

18. Porco - Pig

19. Tomba - Grave or Tomb

20. Rose bianche - White roses

About The Author

Hannah Sarah Abraham is an avid reader, introvert, polyglot and animal lover. She loves writing poems, short stories and novels. She has published several poems in various anthologies and two novels (*T.E.A.R.S.* and *Children of The Dead*). They are available on Amazon. She is currently pursuing an MA in English Literature at AACW (Chennai). Her all-time favourite novel is *The Girl on the Train* by Paula Hawkins.

Other Books By Hannah Sarah Abraham